THE RUSSIAN INTELLIGENCE

Michael Moorcock

Introduced by
Jack Trevor Story

NEW ENGLISH LIBRARY

Copyright © 1980 by Michael Moorcock
Originally published in Great Britain in 1980 by Savoy Books in association with
New English Library.
First published in this edition in 1983 by New English Library, Mill Road, Dunton
Green, Sevenoaks, Kent. Editorial office: 47 Bedford Square, London
WC1B 3DP.

Printed in Great Britain by The Thetford Press Limited, Thetford, Norfolk.

British Library Cataloguing in Publication Data

Moorcock, Michael
    The russian intelligence.
    I. Title

ISBN 0-450-06032-2

Author's Note:
My special thanks to Graham Hall
who helped in the revision from the original (1966)
version of this story.

THROWAWAY FRIENDS

A piece for the front of Michael Moorcock's new novel,
The Russian Intelligence.

Introduction by Jack Trevor Story

The world of Michael Moorcock is an unreal micrososm set
in a terribly actual Marks and Spencer universe. When you
are deeply engrossed and lost to your rotten old mum
(who wants to suckle you really though she calls it just
have your attention for a minute) — right then when you
are escaped, free, hanging on the next lunatic decision,
somebody opens a door and there's Portabello Road.
Christ, what a relief, though, sometimes.

"What is Moorcock getting at?" you have time to think.

His brain is like nothing I have ever seen — and you are
listening to an author who used to be a butcher. I have
seen brains, I have cut them from their cavities, I have
fried them — but nothing like Mike's. It works on its own.
Listen! It works on its own! You watch.

"Hello, Mike — can I come in? I won't if you're busy. I
did knock. I heard you typing from the street. Hilary let
me in." This was his Hilary phase, mother of Max, or so I
believe. We are not friends in that way. No probing. We
know we're not homo-sexual and that's about all we do
know. Well, of course you don't really *know* that. Through
characters like Jerry Cornelius Mike can turn into anything.
I expect that's what he'd doing now — the period was
about then and he hasn't looked round yet. Sitting over
there in the corner banging away on his £500 golf-ball

1

typewriter. Then, from his mouth, his brain probably being in Tokyo, he says:

"Wine behind you, Jack. How are you. Nice of you to call. Any news from Maggie?"

You don't know whether you can talk back or not. Maybe if you talk to his flying fingers. I had done a terrible thing to Maggie and I had to tell him. We are in about 1972/73 and caught in the fury that only true artists know if something non-fiction happens (non-fiction is a monster) — I had come to him for advice. I can't reveal what I had done to Maggie but it was something very personal, committed in a fit of anger that she did not love me any more. Well, that's not absolutely certain, is it?

"Why don't you shoot yourself?" Mike said, his brain still in Tokio and conducting pidgin Japanese because I could see the words coming up on the paper. "Tie a string from the trigger to the door and make your first visitor a murderer — tie the knot so that the gun falls free. Try a short-sheep-shank."

"My God," I thought, "what a friend. How can he help me with my troubles without stopping work?"

And then suddenly you pick up such a book as this one and you understand yet again the qualities that elevate a Michael Moorcock thriller into a land beyond thrillers, the other side of Chandler and Fleming, far, far into the hinterland of THROWAWAY — my own one and only favourite country. Throwaway cliché, throwaway drama, throwaway sentiment, throwaway sex, throwaway throwaway. Mike suddenly ripped the page from the typewriter and threw it away. I now saw the floor — littered with typed pages.

"I hope I haven't spoilt anything, Mike?" I said.

"No! In fact you've helped. I'm trying to light a bonfire in the backyard and I hate burning clean paper. I type all over it first."

By heavens, if only Iris Murdoch could hear this, I

thought. He had now swivelled round towards me and drawn his knees up under his chin so that his heavily bearded face crowned by the cowboy hat evoked for me, irresistibly, Chick Webb, the hunchback drummer of the old Savoy Ballroom days in dear old Harlem.

"You are a cunt, Jack," he said. "What did you want to do that for? Giving away her personal secrets to all her friends and relations and his firm — he'll get the sack! There'll be war with Belgium . . . "

Well, of course it wasn't as bad as that. Mike can't stop inventing. Within the hour I daresay he had another Ladbroke Grove apocalypse. But he had got the main dramatic point which nobody in this country has done. War, I doubt it; but Maggie McDonald has the best reason in the world for fulfilling her vow on the telephone to me from Brussels on the night of October 18th, 1972. She said in her Scottie accents:

"One more word about Paul Nasty and I shall never speak to you again as long as I live . . . "

Of course, that's not his real name. His real name is Waeben. For the television series, Jack On The Box, we called him Mr Nasty. I met him once when I went to 507, Avenue Moliere, Brussels, where Maggie had hidden herself. You can read about it if you go to the British Museum Library at Colindale and look up The Guardian for Saturday July 22 1972 on the Arts Page. To save you a special journey I'll tell you now — she wanted him to stay to dinner with us. She wanted him to help her break the news that I was finished — that it was all over. Oh, he wasn't that nasty I expect — just non-fiction. Rubbish in other words.

"I put you and Maggie into The Chinese Agent, you know," Mike said. Yes, I knew he had. I wish we'd stayed there, really. I was a famous dance band leader and Maggie was a jazz singer. We came out of a posh hotel together, terribly well-dressed, and shall do forever and ever where-ever Michael Moorcock is read and in whatever language. We were crying when Hilary came in with a tray.

"I've brought you some coffee, Jack," she said.

"Thanks, Hilary," I said. Gosh, I'd really like to get her into bed, I thought. And in many other ways Michael Moorcock and I are similar.

PANTHEIST
METAPHYSICIST
SURREALIST
ELYPTICIST
DIAGONALIST
LATERALIST

These are some of the words which have been applied to my writing and to Mike's writing over the past 20 years. Although I started first while we were both working for the Sexton Blake Library and he insists that I inspired him into print — it is Mike who has made most impact as a novelist. Wherever I go I look for my books and can't find them — there's one in Leighton Buzzard public library; wherever I go I find Michael Moorcock. Even right down at Lagos (say it Lahgoosh, like that) in the Cornwall foot of Portugal, so to speak, the one and only isolated German super-market had an entire wall of Michael Moorcock. It makes you sick.

But of course it's nice as well. When Mike won the Guardian Book Prize in 1977 for The Condition Of Muzak (dedicated to me and 23 others) I was able to say:

"I knew him!"

Mike in his formative years was immersed in T. H. White's Once and Future King — that marvellous throwaway history of Arthur and Merlin and the Questing Beast. Now for some links and coincidences. Without ever having heard of White myself my own first novel was compared with The Sword In The Stone by the Chicago Tribune. Why? Because we live in the land of Throwaway — with Fats Waller, with Thornton Wilder, with Twylla Tharp and perhaps with you and you and you. Michael Moorcock, tired of the Sexton Blake routine life of steely eyes and grim forebodings and getting in at nine in the morning, performed the greatest throwaway so far – he threw his typewriter (the firm's) out of a fifth storey window in order to get the sack.

Our editor, Bill Howard Baker, was understandably put out. "You might have killed the wrong person!" he cried. Mike wanted to go and live in Denmark where they have free love. I didn't see him again for something like 15 years. This was perhaps the most fateful, as they say, night of my life. It changed my innocent attitude towards the British police force and the legal system; and this new awareness that Britain is probably the most brain-washed police state in the world is what has motivated in the most profound and fundamental way the intentions (if not the achieve ment) of my writing ever since. And just imagine – this watershed, this crossroads, this shattering and soul-changing experience (without which I would still most probably be writing comedy-thrillers) began on a moment with Maggie and me sitting side by side in the Jaguar at the top of East Heath Road, NW3, wet, dark, cold, two days after Christmas, 1968, I was waiting for traffic to leave a gap so that I could turn right, crossing the top of Heath Street and passing the Whitestone Pond on the way for a drink – possibly at Jack Straw's Castle, probably at The Old Bull and Bush, almost certainly farther out into the country around Harpenden and Bill Johnson.

"Must we always go to Harpenden?" Maggie often said. People say this when you only have one friend.

There was no gap coming so I turned left instead and went down towards Hampstead Village.

"Where we going?" asked Maggie, brightly.

When we came back it was seven in the morning, Sunday morning, without the car, in a taxi, crying, bedraggled, my foot busted by a policeman's boots, Maggie broken in spirit having been stripped in a cell and punched like a

5

punch ball between a gang of policemen – the object being to incite me to rescue her, which I did, or tried to – and it was to cost me £500 to win the appeal squashing her sentence (she was alleged to have kicked a policeman, but I had seen it organised by the sergeant).

"Jack was not drunk," said Hilary Bailey (Mike's wife) in the witness box. "He and Mike had been playing draughts and drinking coffee for two hours since their last drink. We helped him start his car." Hilary and Mike pushing me down Ladbroke Grove at four o'clock in the morning. When I came up to the red light in the deserted streets I was reluctant to wait too long in case the engine stalled – I crept across and the patrol car with one tutor sergeant and three student policemen crept over behind us.

"These old buggers are always the worst," said the sergeant, instructively. And that was just the beginning.

I was on crutches for three months. We began locking our door in case the police came. There was no redress. The Guardian couldn't publish my article about it because of the libel laws in this country – there were ten police witnesses against their two victims.

"I am the best barrister you could find when it comes to cases against the police," said this expensive chap at Lincoln's Inn, "but you would lose the case. The police not only lie but they write their lies down – they are professional liars. You don't stand a chance."

There was also a little regulation that insists you pay a thousand pounds into court before you begin to sue the police for brutality. And also all complaints outside court are investigated by guess who . . . ? The only thing I could do as a writer and remain within the law (I should be a criminal?) was write my next book about a similar incident of police brutality and dedicate it to the policemen involved by name – this I did, the novel: Little Dog's Day. I then wrote another one with the same burst of anger, The Wind In The Snottygobble Tree, which Mike Moorcock published serially in his magazine New Worlds — adding a few sub-stantiating photographs of the author on crutches.

Our new relationship was now bonded with a different kind of cement — we are both serious humourists, serious guitarists, serious throwaway artists. We are both I feel dedicated to enormous erections under which we place our bombs. In The Russian Intelligence Jerry Cornell blows up the rubbish and nonsense of international spying in this see-through transparent world. War is for power and profit — call it patriotism.

What is Patriotism 1979, citizens? Watch my television programme about it this spring.

THE QUEEN APPLAUDS THE HYDROGEN BOMB — ALL'S RIGHT WITH THE WORLD!

Great stuff, this is what keeps us writing, isn't it? You're sixty-two — who needs plots? In Mike's new book, The Russian Intelligence, Jerry's wife knows all this (all our girl friends and wives know all this) and therefore cannot be blamed for fighting all through the book and at the most intensely dramatic nodes of significant action, to get her old man back to bed. Bed is where we belong, citizens, this is where we we we we we WEWEweeeeee — make the future, future, future, future, future, future, future, FUTURE . . .

That sounds a bit like Mike Moorcock, doesn't it? Just a little? And, as I am obsessed with Maggie McDonald of Larkhall, Nr Hamilton, Lanarkshire, Scotland, so my friend Michael Moorcock is obsessed with Derry and Toms. But don't be fooled. Watch the perimeters. This is where it's at with throwaway people.

CHAPTER ONE

The sight of blood was distasteful to Jerry Cornell, even when it wasn't his own.

The sight of a man dying in agony was even more revolting.

Both sights were on today.

The dying man was dressed in a ripped and dusty lounge suit. He lay on a jagged slab of concrete that was part of a bomb site beside the Thames. It was night. It was raining. The lights of London winked on the opposite bank.

The dying man was an acquaintance of Cornell's -- more of a business colleague. A fellow Class A Secret Agent. His name was Thorpe. He was thirty-three, gaunt, red-haired, and had a spiteful tongue.

There was no spite on the tongue now. The tongue moved in the gasping mouth as Thorpe writhed in Cornell's arms and tried to say something. One finger pointed to a heap of tattered paper that had fallen from his pocket. A magazine of some kind.

Cornell shivered and patted Thorpe's shoulder feebly.

"There, there," he said, vaguely. "There, there . . . Don't you worry, Thorpe. An ambulance is on its way."

Thorpe was trying desperately to communicate with him. If Cornell had been doing his job properly he would have listened carefully. But the whole episode was so unpleasant he didn't want to do anything at all. He certainly didn't want to hold a dying man in his arms. The rain was ruining his suit and so was Thorpe's blood.

Sounds began to come from Thorpe's throat. They were extremely ugly sounds. Cornell wished he would shut up and get on with dying.

The sounds became clearer, but Cornell still couldn't make out the sense.

"Is inners trip," Thorpe said. Or perhaps it was "Its innards drip," or maybe "Its inner trip."

"Don't talk now," Cornell said with an effort.

Obediently, Thorpe stopped talking. He shuddered once and then went limp.

With a sigh of relief, Cornell realised that Thorpe was dead. He let go of the body and laid it on the slab. He stood up and looked down at Thorpe's mangled face. Someone had given the agent a real going over. He had been tortured to death.

Above him, on the bridge that flanked the bomb site, cars drew up. Cornell saw the white body and flashing lights of an ambulance. Figures began to descend the steep sides of the bomb site and stumble through the silvered darkness towards him.

The man in the lead was very small, almost petite. Cornell recognised him as the boss - - Commander Fry, Chief of Cell 87. His pale face was pudgy and grim. The eyes, as ever, were slightly shifty and anxious.

"Hello, Jerry," he said. "How's Thorpe?"

"Gone to the Big Cell in the Sky," Cornell said, tasting bile in his mouth.

The remark was lost on Fry. He patted Cornell's arm sympathetically. "Don't take it hard, Jerry. Poor Thorpe. Tough. Very tough."

Cornell turned away, impatient with Fry's predictable sentiments.

The ambulancemen began to dump the corpse onto their stretcher.

Cornell walked some distance from them and stood looking down into the oily river. Fry joined him.

"Did he - - did he say anything, Jerry? Before he died?"

"Nothing that made any sense," Cornell replied. "Something that sounded like 'Its innards drip'. He said it several times."

He liked Fry less than usual for bothering him. He wanted to go home to his wife Shirley and get her to pour him a drink while he had a bath. Then he would make love to her and forget the disgusting Thorpe and his disgusting death.

"Maybe it was some sort of code," Fry said thoughtfully. "Its innards drip - - might have something to do with the inner part of a machine. I don't know."

"Maybe." Cornell began to walk back across the bomb site. The ambulancemen were taking Thorpe up to the bridge. Several other men were standing around, flashing torches over the ground. One of them picked up the tattered magazine Thorpe had pointed at.

He shone his torch on it. Fry reached out and took it from him, looking at it curiously.

"Thorpe had that with him when I found him," Cornell said.

"It's a comic," Fry murmured in surprise. "A kid's comic. Funny thing for Thorpe to be carrying round. He was always strong on the heavy stuff - - the classics."

"Everyone's got to relax," Cornell said bitterly. "Sometime."

Fry straightened the pages and looked at the title. "Whoomf," he said.

"What was that, sir?" asked the man who had found the comic.

"*Whoomf!* - - that's the name. What a curious title."

"They're all called things like that these days, sir," said the man, knowledgeably. He had three kids. *"Blam - - Splat - - Kerrunch* - - you know the sort of thing, sir."

"Too much violence altogether," Fry muttered half to himself. "We used to have papers called *Magnet, Gem* and *Pluck.* A damn' sight healthier if you ask me."

"Thorpe was pointing to it," Cornell told his chief. "Pointed at it while he was saying whatever he was saying."

"Could be a clue, I suppose," Fry said.

11

"Could be, sir," said the man who had found it.

Fry handed it back to him. "Hang on to it then, would you? Turn it over to the lab boys."

"Right-ho, sir."

"You'd better keep searching the area for anything else," Fry told the man. "Do what you can. I know it won't be easy in this weather at night."

"Right-ho, sir."

"I'll be at the office if you want me," Fry said. "Come on, Jerry."

They walked back over the rubble, clambered up the muddy sides of the site and reached the bridge. Fry opened the door of his black Daimler but didn't get in.

"You got here about half-an-hour ago and couldn't find Thorpe. Is that right?" he asked Cornell. "He phoned you last night. Said he was on to something. Told you to meet him here tonight." These weren't questions. Jerry had already reported it all. "You looked for Thorpe and did finally find him - - dying?"

No, selling used cars, Cornell felt like answering. Instead he agreed wearily.

"That's right, commander."

"Hmmm," said Fry.

Cornell cleared his throat, trying not to sound too much like Thorpe's last words. "Er. . . I'm a bit tired, sir."

"Of course you are, Jerry." Fry looked up and gave Cornell an encouraging smile. "You've had a rough time. Thorpe wasn't a pretty sight."

"He was a very nasty sight, sir. I hope I never see another like it. There's nothing more for me to do tonight - - can I go home?"

"Of course." Fry ducked to get into his car. "See you in the morning. Maybe by that time the lab will be able to tell us what connection a kid's comic has with a serious leakage of secrets."

Cornell walked away. He didn't care what the connection

12

was. He suspected there wasn't one; there hardly ever was in a case like this - - or any other case Jerry had been coerced to work on. His own opinion was that Thorpe was a closet comic reader. He opened the door of his Armstrong-Siddely, slid into the engulfing leather seat and started the car.

He resented Thorpe for phoning him and not the office in the first place. He resented him for making the appointment to meet at a bomb site. He resented him most of all for turning up there in such a disgusting condition.

It had ruined his evening.

Jerry U-turned on the bridge. A taxi whizzed by, honking.

He drove north, back towards his flat in Notting Hill.

As he neared his traditional stamping grounds, Cornell's spirits rose a little. This kind of thing didn't happen very often, especially if you went out of your way to avoid it. Philosophically, he decided that you had to put up with the occasional nasty experience if you wanted to keep a job as cushy as his. And, after all, the secret agent business was a pretty cushy business to be in for most of the agents most of the time.

Most of the time.

CHAPTER TWO

GIVEN HALF A chance, there was little doubt that Jerry Cornell would have settled down to married life as one to the manner born.

Subconsciously, he craved respectability — pipe-and-slippers evenings by the telly, a semi in the suburbs, a lawn to mow, Sunday outings in a Cortina to Brighton, Hampstead Heath or Box Hill. The works.

Cornell resisted the craving. He told himself that such a life was boring, meaningless and — much more important — unfashionable.

A romantic soul, Jerry Cornell could easily have fallen completely in love with his wife Shirley and convinced himself that the Secret Service business was glamorous and important.

As a Class A Secret Agent he knew his trade wasn't glamorous. He knew too it was hardly ever important. No matter what effort you put in to stop Secret X reaching Country Z, it got there sooner or later. Generally sooner. Russia knew everything Klaus Fuchs or the Rosenbergs or Burgess and Maclean had to tell them long before they were unmasked. The business of getting one side to defect to another was mostly just a matter of public relations, like transferring a top football star from Liverpool to Chelsea.

The spy trade was, on the whole, a different kind of game — but it was a game, nonetheless. That was how Jerry Cornell saw it. And he should have known.

The one thing that saved the spy business, in his opinion, was that it was decidedly fashionable — even camp. He, Jerry Cornell, was — according to the Sunday Supplements

— a modern myth-hero, the direct spiritual descendant of Ulysses, Robin Hood and Buffalo Bill — and maybe even Jack the Ripper, too (he was never quite sure what constituted a myth-hero, modern or otherwise).

Of course, another saving grace was that it offered a splendid opportunity for skiving and fiddling.

It was much like the army in that respect — only better. Not working regular hours, he could exaggerate the time jobs took him (if he did them at all) and, requiring fairly hefty expenses, he could exaggerate how much he'd had to spend (if he spent anything).

Not that spying was his choice of profession. He'd been shanghaied into it because of his facility for languages; his somewhat typical appearance; his air of Cornellian fecklessness and seediness (which helped him merge in almost anywhere the feckless and the seedy gathered, especially betting shops and large railway stations), — and because if he hadn't joined they would have put him in prison for a long, long time for various things they knew — and could prove — he had done (including desertion from the army). And they still could put him inside if he didn't toe the line.

Jerry was a bit of a bum, really. He had his good points but, like a championship Old English sheepdog, he managed to keep them hidden most of the time.

Shirley Cornell (nee Garmon, his wife of three months) loved him, but then again she was a bit of a fool, like most women. She believed his job was glamorous and important. She also believed everything Jerry told her — except one. She couldn't believe he was faithful to her.

She was right.

Jerry pursued infidelity with the same determination that makes other men change the course of history. He felt that faithfulness had no place in his character. To be faithful was to lose any integrity he possessed. To be faithful was to sell out his ideals. He was fanatically unfaithful. His infidelity caused him pain, misery, inconvenience,

16

heavy expenses and hardly any pleasure at all. But he soldiered on. Infidelity was his creed — ultimate unfaithfulness his goal.

It was probably the only justification he could make for his marriage to Shirley. It had happened shortly after the Kung Fu Tzu case* when, badly demoralised by the events that had taken place around him, he had found himself proposing to Shirley, then receptionist at National Insurance (the cover firm for Cell 87).

It was a classic case of opposites attract.

Shirley was dedicated to her own ideal. She was grimly determined to scotch all Jerry's attempts at infidelity by any means within her grasp, even if it involved as much effort as Jerry put into those attempts. No trouble was too great. He wasn't going to flit from flower to flower while she was holding the bug spray in one beringed hand.

And Jerry had already discovered what Shirley could do. On three separate occasions he had dropped in at his latest pick-up's flat only to find that Shirley had called before him and frightened the girl off.

He could never find out exactly what it was that Shirley said that frightened them so much. Their lips were sealed. Whenever he referred to her, their eyes went wild and their mouths trembled. Little mewling sounds would come from their lips and their faces would turn very pale.

Jerry was driving very slowly home. He took his special short route there. It involved crossing a red light and going the wrong way up two one-way streets. He hesitated once as he passed a block of flats in the King's Road. There was a girl that he'd met two nights previously at the Mandrake Club. Then he thought of Shirley and decided to go on home.

There probably wasn't much point in stopping off.

He didn't bother to put the Armstrong-Siddely in the garage. He left it outside his flat and walked wearily up the steps. He hoped Shirley wasn't in a fighting mood. He was

*See THE CHINESE AGENT

17

too tired for that. All he wanted was comforting after his ordeal at the bomb-site. And maybe a little bit more.

Shirley was waiting for him in the living room.

Her glossy black hair was styled in the short late-20's look. She was wearing a green silk mini-dress that showed all of her wonderful legs and emphasised the rest of her admirable figure admirably. Her big, bright, brown eyes were warm and her oval face wore a lovely smile.

He was safe.

"Hello, Jerry. What did Thorpe have to say?"

Cornell shrugged. "Some garbled sentence over and over again. He's dead now. Whoever got hold of him tortured him to death — probably thought they'd finished him off. I'll never know how he made it to the bomb site."

"Oh, dear. How nasty. Sit down and I'll bring you a drink."

Cornell was in a passive mood. "Make it a big pint mug of cocoa," he said. "All milk."

"Right you are darling." Shirley drifted gracefully into the kitchen.

Cornell took off his jacket and hung it over one of the upright chairs by the table. He unbuckled his shoulder holster and hung the gun over the jacket. He loosened his tie and undid his collar. As he went to sit down he looked at his trousers and noticed that they still had Thorpe's blood on them.

With a shiver he went into the bedroom and took off his trousers. He put on a pair of jeans and returned to the living room.

Shirley came in with the cocoa.

"Did Thorpe seem to know anything about who's leaking all that secret information from Whitehall?" she asked. "Did he find out how the information's being passed?"

Cornell shook his head. He was only indirectly involved with the case. It had been Thorpe's pigeon, and Thorpe was a much better agent than he was (though Fry didn't know that). In Thorpe's position Jerry would have made a great show of tracking down some unlikely-looking lead, but would really have done nothing much more than spend a few days out of town, tooling around in the country. It was easy enough to fake reports on a job like that. Usually, given enough time, the traitor gave himself away and the case was 'solved.'

Fry would doubtless turn this case over to Jerry in the morning. And Jerry wouldn't make the same mistake that Thorpe obviously had of actually uncovering some real information. Always a silly thing to do. Look what happened to you when you did.

Cornell grabbed Shirley as soon as he'd finished his cocoa. He really needed comforting.

CHAPTER THREE

NEXT MORNING Jerry Cornell took the tube to work. He went from Notting Hill Gate station to the Bank. Lost in a crowd of bowler hats and headscarves, he made his way through Old Lombard Place until he turned into Christopher Street which led to Shepherd's Lane. The narrow lane ran between two tall, gloomy warehouses and led to Rash Court.

In the middle of the towering sooty cliffs, that were run-down offices and warehouses there stood a little building that had been built fairly recently. It was a cheerful little building, painted bright red and trimmed with white; the doors and window frames were yellow and the iron hinges a shining black. Roses — yellow and purple — grew in the blue flower box in front of the windows which were covered by venetian blinds.

In flowing script on a brass plate screwed to the door were the words: NATIONAL INSURANCE (Registered Offices). Only a few select people knew that the insurance firm was the headquarters of an even less noble enterprise — Cell 87 of British Security.

In the reception cubicle that had once been occupied by Shirley Garmon another girl glanced brightly up at Cornell. She was a honey blonde with wasp-coloured eyes and a bee-sting mouth. She looked scared for a moment when she recognised him. A shadow crossed her eyes as she seemed to remember something unspeakable. Hildebrand Hastings-Lyndon (for that was her name) was one of the young women who had received a visit from her predecessor.

"Fry available?" Cornell asked curtly. Since their last — and final — date he had always been somewhat hostile

21

towards Hildebrand. Would true love — or even lust — let a threat or two stand in its path?

Hildebrand's honey-coloured hair swung as she turned to her switchboard and buzzed Commander Robert Fry's office.

"Mr. Cornell to see you, sir," said Hildebrand to the receiver. She nodded and, without turning back, said: "He'll see you now, Mr. Cornell."

Cornell crossed the little hall to the door on the left marked 'Managing Director'. Without knocking, he walked in. His chief, tiny and anxious, a few strands of grey hair carefully brushed across his bald dome, sat behind a desk that was too big for him. Cornell noticed that his feet didn't touch the ground. Cornell sat down in the deep armchair facing the desk.

"Morning, Jerry," Fry said. He looked as if he had been up all night. He probably *had* been up all night.

Cornell hated Fry's familiar use of his first name. There wasn't much he could do about it though, except discomfort Fry in subtle ways. Like making no reply.

"Morning," Fry repeated vaguely, sensing that something was wrong but unable to work out what it was. When a man automatically expected courtesy, the smallest discourtesy could faze him.

On Fry's desk was a copy of *Whoomf!* It was a new copy, not the one Cornell had seen the night before. It was the same issue, by the look of it. Fry picked it up by the edges and handed it across the desk to Cornell who stretched forward to take it.

"See anything special about it, Jerry?"

Cornell riffled through the pages. There were the usual gory war stories, space stories, vaguely supernatural stories, sports stories, all in strip form. Some were in colour, some weren't. The leading strip, in colour on the front and back pages, was called *The Devil Rider — Masked Fighter for Justice.* It seemed to be about a character in a fantastic

22

mask and medieval gear who rode about the East Anglia countryside in the old smuggling days righting wrongs. Cornell remembered similar stories from his own boyhood. Nothing changed much in the comic business.

"I'm not an authority on comics, sir," he said when he'd found nothing extraordinary about the paper. "Should I see anything special?"

"I'm not sure. The lab people found little marks that Thorpe had apparently made — on that front page strip — in some of the balloons. But why he did it — if he did it — I don't know."

Cornell looked at some of the dialogue.

STAND BACK, DEVIL RIDER — OR I BLOW YOU TO PERDITION, said a periwigged gentleman, waving a horse pistol. Several redcoats stood uncertainly behind him.

HA! SIR MONTAGUE DARES DEFY THE DEVIL RIDER, smirked the fantastically masked hero, pointing a finger at the man in the periwig. THEN SUFFER THE DEVIL RIDER'S DARK VENGEANCE!

The next picture showed a streak of lightning leaving the Devil Rider's finger and sizzling Sir Montague's periwig, making his soldiers laugh. Sir Montague's balloon said: 'YEEEEE-AAAAARGH-GAAAAAR!" The soldiers shared a balloon that read: "HA! HA! HA!" and the Devil Rider's balloon said: "THERE'S A TASTE OF MY WRATH, WICKED OPPRESSOR OF THE POOR!"

The Devil Rider didn't seem to indulge in much real violence, Cornell noted. He wondered where the lightning came from to power his fingers.

"It's just a comic strip, sir. I don't think it means much. We're on the wrong track."

Fry pursed his lips and looked self-consciously thoughtful. "No," he said slowly. "I've got a hunch, Jerry. I think this really something to do with the case. I'd like you to take it on."

Cornell still believed the comic strip angle was useless,

but was quite happy to chase red herrings while the real fish escaped — especially if he was only following orders. It would make for a nice, quiet job with no problems. When the transfer season came around again, the traitors who were passing secrets out of Whitehall would give themselves away as they invariably did, the case would be 'solved' and Cornell would have avoided Thorpe's unpleasant fate.

"I suppose you're right, sir," he said with renewed interest. "Yes — that comic could be the clue we need. I see what you mean now."

A look of faint puzzlement crossed Fry's weary face. "Glad you think so, Jerry. Any ideas where to start?"

"I thought I might make a tour of the Fleet Street pubs, sir, to see if I can find anything out about the editor of the comic and so on . . . "

It was a nice try. Inadvertently, Fry scotched it.

"No, we'll try the direct method, Jerry. Go straight to Wayflete Publications in Great Pie Street — that's the road that intersects Fleet Street at the top of Ludgate Hill. They're the publishers."

Cornell sighed. "All right, sir."

"I'll tell you what I think the connection is," Fry said after a pause. "It was how Thorpe died, d'you see?"

Cornell felt uncomfortable. He wished Fry hadn't brought that subject up.

"Oh, really?" he said faintly.

He reached into his inside pocket, took out a cigarette case and lighted a fag. He inhaled heavily.

"Yes," Fry pressed on. "The way the poor fellow died. He was tortured to death."

"I know, sir."

"It was ritual murder by torture, Jerry — know what I mean?"

"No, sir . . . " Cornell was trying not to listen.

"Ritual torture — the sort of thing devil worshippers do to people in Haiti and places — and here, from time to time."

"Ah . . . " There was something unhealthy, Cornell decided, about Fry's dwelling on the subject. He hoped that his chief had finished. But Fry continued.

"Well, you see the connection now, don't you, Jerry? Devil worshippers — the Devil Rider. It all fits."

Cornell shuddered. Surely there couldn't really be a connection? Surely he hadn't allowed himself to get involved with a case where there was real danger!

His legs were a little shaky as he stood up.

"Be careful, Jerry," Fry said grimly. He left the desk and took Cornell's hand in a firm grip. "Be very careful."

Jerry intended to be. He squared his jaw and put on his heroic expression (itself borrowed from the comics of his youth.) It always impressed Fry, he knew.

"Don't worry, sir. I will," he said. "But when a job's got to be done, it's got to be done. A man knows deep down inside what he has to do in a case like this." John Wayne would've been proud of him. Cornell smiled frostily. A beautiful phrase occurred to him. He gave it to Fry, complete with a slight catch in the throat. "I'll find those beggars who got poor Thorpe, sir. I'll bring them to book — if — if it's the last thing I do, sir. They can't do a thing like that to one of us and get away with it."

"I know how you feel, Jerry," Fry murmured, tightening his grip on Cornell's hand. "But don't — don't do anything foolish, will you? Look after yourself — you're one of our best men, y'know." He laughed embarrassedly. "We don't want to lose another A-Class agent, do we?"

Cornell echoed the laugh.

"No, sir," he said, with some feeling.

Fry wasn't half sentimental, he thought. It was all right when it came to conning him, but the trouble with sentimental people was that they tended to involve you in somewhat prolonged scenes of this type — particularly when you were shaking with terror at the thought of being

25

tortured to death by devil worshippers. He couldn't hold out much longer. He wanted to go to the bathroom. Badly.

Fry brought his left hand over and clasped Cornell's. He began to pump the limp arm up and down.

"Keep in touch with H.Q., Jerry."

"I will, sir. Um — about expenses." Luckily reason prevailed through the welter of emotion. "Expenses, sir — they'll be quite heavy, I should think."

"I'll give you a chitty."

"Thank you, sir."

"Remember our budget's a bit tight, what with the new government's restrictions," Fry said, still pumping Cornell's hand.

"I will, sir."

"I'll give you a chitty, then." ·

Cornell felt like weeping. How long was it going to last?

"Thank you, sir."

Finally Fry let go of Cornell's hand and went over to his desk. He took out a pad, scribbled illegibly on it and signed.

"There it is," he said, handing the chitty to Cornell.

Cornell grasped it, muttered something inarticulate and staggered from the room.

Fry stood watching him leave. Cornell didn't show much on the surface, he thought, but he's determined to track down the traitors, you can tell. Cornell was brave — maybe even a little reckless — but he was dedicated to his job. If anyone could bring the traitors to book, Cornell could.

Outside Fry's office, Cornell was leaning against the wall, wiping sweat from his face. There *couldn't* be any real connection between the comic strip and the devil worshippers, he thought. If he got even so much as a whisper that there was, he was going to make very sure he stayed clear of whoever it was that had done whatever was done to Thorpe.

CHAPTER FOUR

IN HIS old-fashioned man-about-town-of-1959 suit with its two vents, waisted jacket and narrow trousers. Jerry Cornell fitted very wel' into the Fleet Street scene. He only needed a bow tie and a yellow waistcoat to look like any one of any hundred journalists or advertising men who thronged the street. His hair was fairly long, fairly greasy: his skin seemed to possess a faint film of oily grime, he was quite good-looking in a rather weak sort of way. It was incredible how many there were who looked just like him. Cornell didn't realise it, of course, and neither did they.

The street of ink was also the street of burks and herberts, talentless bums and the talented conmen who do very well possessing no other talent but that. Behind the walls of the newspaper offices, twenty men did inefficiently what one man could have done efficiently (if a man of some talent existed); milling in the streets men and women bustled about on useless errands. In the pubs and restaurants, similar men and women who realised how useless their occupations were simply sat and ate and drank and gossiped. Fleet Street was also the street of gossip.

Malice flowed through it from the Law Courts at one end to Ludgate Hill at the other. Petty malice mainly. It was a sour street. A street of failures. Most of the people who had anything in them still had left it years before.

It was a street of inaccuracies; a street of outright lies. The conmen who propagated the inaccuracies and lies were the best kinds of conmen — they believed their own stories. There was no-one more gullible than a Fleet Street reporter. Though his own mind and life were of the most conventional, he. would swallow any fantastic tale you

27

cared to give him. What was worse — if the public read it in his newspaper, they would believe it too. They wouldn't believe the man in the pub if he told it to them, but they would believe the story if they read it in their favourite daily. Yet half the time it was the man in the pub who told the reporter who then told the public.

Thus there is reality and reality. The reality of existence superseded, overwhelmed, destroyed, by the reality of the printed page.

Jerry Cornell moved through the crowds of fantasists and deceivers unaware that he was surrounded by black magicians, acolytes of a mysterious creature whose object was to feed illusion to the human race until it could no longer distinguish the lie from the truth. Magazines, news-papers and advertising agencies — all dedicated to the same end: The Ultimate Faze.

The agent turned left just before Ludgate Hill and entered Great Pie Street which was dominated by a mon-strous multi-levelled, glaring white building sloganned in blazing blue neon pronouncing the words:

WAYFLETE PUBLICATIONS
WAYFLETE MAGAZINES ARE
A WAY OF LIFE!
WAYFLETE MAGAZINES ARE
HAPPY MAGAZINES!
WAYFLETE MAGAZINES ARE
WHOPPERS!
WAYFLETE MAGAZINES ARE
WAY OUT AHEAD!

Bowing his head before this sky-filling exaltation. Jerry Cornell entered the lobby of the world's biggest comic publishers and was greeted by a bored-looking doorman who sat by a display of some fifty comics, women's maga-zines and assorted periodicals that had in common only the fact that they were cheaply written, cheaply printed on cheap paper and probably each made a million pounds a year profit.

The bored-looking doorman was actually reading a copy of *Whoomf!* when Jerry Cornell came in. He put it down without reluctance and ambled across to the agent.

"Yes, sir?"

"I want to talk to the editor of *Whoomf!*" Cornell told him. "Can I do that?"

"What's your name, sir? What do you do?"

"Arnold," Cornell lied for the sake of it. "Matt Arnold. I'm a poet. I know a bit about painting too. I thought I might be able to write for your comics, you see."

"Poet, eh?"

"In advertising."

"Ah!" The doorman seemed to approve. "The jingles! On the telly! Har, har, har, har! Which ones are yours?"

"The dirty ones," Cornell told him, smiling weakly.

"What was the name again?"

"Arnold — Arnold Swinburne."

The doorman went to a desk in a jungle of potted plants and picked up a phone. He dialled a numer.

"Mr. Wharton," he said. "Yes please." He put his hand over the speaker. "They're putting him through, sir." He paused, listening importantly. "Ah — Mr. Wharton? Ah! A Mr. Harold Gwynn-Burne to see you, sir. 'E's a writer, I gather. You busy, sir? Righto, then, yes. Ah! Yes."

The doorman put the phone down and winked at Cornell.

"You're okay. You can go up. Know the number?"

Cornell shook his head.

"Har, har, har!" said the doorman, putting his lips together and making a barely heard sputtering sound with them. "Neither do I! Sppttttttt."

He went back to the phone and picked up a book beside it. "Here it is, sir. Room 909. That's the ninth floor. Take the lift up, sir. Good luck with them jingles. Sppttt."

Cornell went to one of the four lifts and pressed the UP

button.

When he got to the ninth floor, Cornell found himself in the centre of a corridor that looked more like a long hospital corridor than anything else. It was white on ceiling, walls and doors. There was grey springy rubber surfacing the floors. The corridor was deserted.

He looked at the notice in front of him. It said:

NOS: 900-950

and an arrow pointed left.

NOS: 951-998

and an arrow pointed right.

Cornell turned left.

He walked along the corridor until it slanted round and branched into two. Here he followed arrows until he reached a door that was exactly the same as all the others save that it had the number 909 on it and the words MANAGING EDITOR, B. Wharton. *Do not enter.*

Cornell turned the handle and entered, glad of the opportunity.

Suddenly something slammed on to his head. He staggered against the wall, clutching his head and looking at the objects which had fallen on him. A pile of big encyclopedias. Somehow they had been balanced over the door to fall on his head when he opened it. A booby-trap! A schoolboy's booby-trap!

"Ha! Ha! Ha!" came a merry laugh from somewhere by the window.

Cornell blinked and peered at the big desk and the big man who sat at it, his back to the window.

"Oh, I say, ha, ha, ha! What a wheeze! Oh, dear, he, he, he, what a super jape. Oooh! He, he, he! S-sorry, old chap — but it did say d-don't enter, didn't it? Oh ha, ha, ha, oh, ha, ha, ha — you d-deserved it r-rather!"

The man with the Billy Bunter dialogue must have been over fifty. His hair was grey. He was fat and wore rimless glasses. He was convulsed with laughter.

"You're j-jolly lucky it wasn't *flour*, he, he, he!" he said, wiping his eyes. "It was flour last time."

Cornell rubbed his head and sighed. "Flour, eh? At least it would have been a damn' sight softer. You could kill someone like that."

"Oh, I say, no — you don't think so. It's only a bit of fun."

"Are you Mr Barry Wharton?" Cornell asked, stepping over the books and approaching the desk.

"I am. You're the chap wanting to do some scripts for us, I understand."

"That's right." Cornell had decided he might get more information in the role of would-be writer than any of the other guises he might choose.

"Hmmm — it's a hard thing to do, you know. Takes a lot of skill. Not many people are capable of comic-strip writing, did you know that?"

"No, I didn't . . . "

"It's an art form of its own, you know," Wharton said seriously. "We get loads of people in who think they can write scripts — but out of every hundred only one can deliver what we want. Think of that. That's one per cent. What have you done?"

"Radio scripts — a few television scripts," Cornell lied. "But mainly I've written advertising stuff — jingles, features for trade magazines, that sort of thing."

Wharton's strange, old-young face with its pink, pudgy skin and its grey hair, looked doubtful. "Not really our line." He waved towards a cushioned chair opposite him. "Sit down, anyway."

As Cornell sat down, the cushion went *fffrrrrrrtttt*. Wharton giggled. Cornell managed a pale smile. He kept a wary eye on Wharton's lapel where an artificial flower reposed. When they were retarded at Wayflete Publications they were really retarded, he decided.

31

Wharton leaned across the desk.

"Smell that," he said, pushing the flower at Cornell.

"No, I don't . . . "

Cornell noticed Wharton's features hardening. With the air of a martyr he decided that he'd better go along with Wharton. He put his nose to the flower and waited for the water to shoot up it. It shot up. He coughed, spluttered, wiped his nose and sat back, grinning like a corpse with double rigor mortis. Wharton was in fits.

When the giggling, snorting and other noises had subsided. Cornell said: "Could you tell me about the comic itself, Mr Wharton — *Whoomf!* I mean."

"*Whoomf!* is only one of many comics I control, Mr — er — "

"Bunter," Cornell said. "William Bunter."

A big smile spread across Wharton's face. "Oh, I say, not really — Bunter! Bunter and Wharton, eh? Know what I'm talking about?"

Cornell did. That was why he'd chosen the name.

"Of course!" he said in an amazed tone. "The good old *Magnet* — Greyfriars School and all that!"

"What a joke! Do they call you Billy? You haven't really got the figure for the name, have you?"

Cornell shook his head.

Wharton laughed and shouted in merriment for what seemed several hours. He spluttered at Cornell, come round and clapped Cornell on the back, pumped Cornell's hand. When it began to subside, Cornell said:

"About these scripts, then . . . "

"What would you like to do?" Wharton said with a warm, friendly smile.

"Well, I thought I'd have a go at the Devil Rider strip . . . " Cornell began.

Wharton pursed his lips. "Jolly sorry, old chap — no can do. Much as I'd like to. Y'see we've got a regular writer for that."

"Who's that?" Cornell asked innocently.

"We don't disclose names of other writers — saves a lot of jealously and so on. How about doing a spec job on Martinson's Marines — war stuff?" Wharton picked up a copy of *Whoomf!* and turned a few pages before spreading it out before Cornell. *Martinson's Marines* were, it appeared, schoolboys involved in winning the war against the Japanese in the East Indies.

"How much do you pay for these?" Cornell asked.

"About fifteen guineas for fourteen frames or so," Wharton said. "Sorry it can't be more."

Cornell was thinking that maybe there was a better and easier racket than the spy game after all!

Wharton glanced at his watch. "I say — it's coming up for break time. How about a noggin or two over at the Black Swan? That's where we all gather. Shouldn't think you'd be averse to a few sandwiches either, eh — *Bunter?* Ho, ho, ho!"

Cornell rose wearily from his chair. He could certainly do with a drink, he agreed.

CHAPTER FIVE

JUDY JUDD was a very vivacious redhead. She sat in the pub surrounded by the staff of *Whoomf!* If anyone had *whoomf*, Judy Judd had it. Jerry Cornell had already bought her three large gins and tonic and was in the process of buying her another. He stared at her glassily and she smiled back warmly. She was editor of *Teen Scream*, Wayflete's top selling pop music paper. She wore a pair of Mick Jagger hipsters, Cilla Black earrings, and a sweater stretched on her ample bosom which said 'Let's Frug Tonite'. Perched on her Sandy Shaw coiffure was a neat little Donovan cap and on her feet were red, white and blue Who-shoes. Judy Judd really lived her work — or dressed it, anyway.

If she possessed a flaw (and Jerry Cornell was prepared to overlook it) it was that her vocabulary was somewhat limited.

"'Nother drink?" he asked hotly.

"Great!" she said.

"Same again?" he said, waving to the barman.

"Fabulous!" said Judy Judd.

He ordered the drink and handed it to her.

"Wild!" she said, by way of thanks.

Barry Wharton was telling some infantile joke to his staff. They rolled about in carefully simulated mirth. Oblivious of the noise, Cornell stared into Judy Judd's mascaraed eyes.

"Do you enjoy your work, Judy?" he breathed.

"Swinging!" she breathed back. "Absolutely the end, you know. Crazy!"

If there was something artificial about Judy Judd's

vocabulary, perhaps she couldn't be blamed. The one thing Wayflete Publications demanded of its editorial staff was that they should be dedicated. Doubtless these people began life as perfectly ordinary men and women, but a few years at Wayflete and they began to live their work. That probably explained Barry Wharton's juvenile japes and schoolboy vocabulary. Barry Wharton irritated Jerry Cornell. Judy Judd didn't. She stimulated him.

"You're a script-writer, are you?" she asked him. "Sounds a rave!"

"I hope to do some," he said. "I wanted to do the Devil Rider, but I gather that's already booked to someone else."

She laughed suddenly. "Yes — I flipped — I really did — when I heard who was doing it."

"I thought his name was kept a secret?" Cornell wasn't really interested, but he did want to keep the conversation with Judy going.

"Well, I suppose it is — no wonder! It's positively *groovey*. He — "

Barry Wharton had turned up by the bar where Judy sat on her stool. He leaned over Cornell. "I say, Bunter, is your postal order here yet? Haw, haw, haw!"

Cornell shifted uncomfortably and produced a watery smile. "Not yet, Wharton — I suppose you couldn't lend me a fiver till it does?"

Wharton shook with helpless laughter. "That's it!" he spluttered. "That's it! Ho, ho, ho!"

Judy Judd raised a magnificent eyebrow. Cornell tried to shrug at her without Wharton noticing. He was feeling desperate. It was almost closing time and he wanted to make a date with Judy before it was too late.

Wharton moved down the bar to order more pints. "Got to get the last round in before the tuck shop shuts, eh?" he said over his shoulder. "He, he, he!"

"Are you doing anything tonight?" Cornell asked Judy Judd, throwing the soft approach away as time ticked by.

She looked crestfallen. "No! I'm absolutely *down*. I was going to The Secretary Bird in Wardour Street — they've got this fabulous group on tonight — but my boy-friend can't make it."

"Maybe I could take you?" Cornell suggested quickly. "I could pick you up after work. I've never been to The Secretary Bird — is it good?"

"The most," she said. "The absolute end. The group's too much! The Wilful Mad — have you heard them?"

"No, but I'd love to," Cornell said with a shudder.

"Oh — then it's my duty to take *you* there. Yes — meet me at six o'clock in here, okay?"

"Okay." Cornell congratulated himself that this was one date Shirley wasn't going to break up. She knew he was on a job. He could easily phone her and tell her it was taking him out of town.

The pub bell rang. Barry Wharton approached Cornell.

"Well, Bunter — I hope you can do us a sample script soon, old chap." Wharton clapped Cornell heavily on the back. "Have a go — and we'll see you in a few days, eh?"

"Wizard!" said Cornell, inspired.

When Wharton had left the pub, followed by his gang, Jerry and Judy lingered for a moment. She smiled at him sexily. "I must zoom," she said. "See you later."

"Fabulous!" he said.

He watched her leave, then turned to the bar. He might as well phone Shirley right away and give her his story. The barman directed him to the phone. He dialled his flat's number. Shirley answered almost immediately.

"Hello, Shirley. Look — I think I'm on to something. I've got to go out of town. May not be back tonight. Okay?

She hesitated. "Okay, Jerry — you're not up to anything, are you?"

"No time for that, darling," he told her.

37

"All right, then — oh, there was a message for you. From Commander Fry. Will you phone the office."

"What was it about?"

"No idea," she said.

"Okay. Thanks. See you tomorrow."

"Look after yourself." She hung up.

Cornell stood by the phone for a moment wondering whether to pretend he hadn't got Shirley's message or not. Then he decided that if they phoned his flat again they would soon discover she had given him the message.

He dialled the office number.

He got through to Fry.

"Ah, Jerry — any lead?"

"I'm not sure, sir. I'm trying to find out who's writing the Devil Rider strip — but they seem to be covering up."

"Keep at it, Jerry. Listen, we had someone else check the subscription list of *Whoomf!* Guess what we found out?"

"What, sir?"

"One of the copies goes to a Fydor Dyescheoffski in Kensington!"

"A Russian!" Jerry said dynamically.

"Quite so. I want you to go over there now, Jerry — play it cool, eh — but see what you can find out about this Dyescheoffski's connection with the comic. There's a Dyescheoffski works at the Russian Embassy, so the link between the comic and the secrets we're losing could be even stronger than we thought." Fry gave Cornell the full address — a house in Ladbroke Road, quite close to Cornell's own flat.

Cornell thought of the story he'd given Shirley.

"Er — do I have to get over there today, sir . . . ?"

"This is urgent, Jerry. The sooner the better."

Silently cursing, Cornell replaced the receiver.

He left the pub and walked back up Fleet Street to Aldwych where he'd parked the Armstrong-Siddely.

He took his time heading for Kensington.

CHAPTER SIX

JOSEPH K. SAT back in the shadows of the garret room, a bulky, menacing figure in heavy black overcoat and black homburg hat. He had the pale, lugubrious face of a New England undertaker. His white shirt was very white and the knot of his tasteful tie very correctly tied.

The man who had the misfortune to be called Pyotr Zhivako (and thus been the subject of much rib-nudging in Moscow and at the Embassy in London due to the Pasternak scandal) knew that Joseph K. carried a heavy, old-fashioned Luger in a shoulder holster under his left arm. He also knew that Joseph K. was perhaps the very last of a certain school of officials who had been trained under Stalin and this made Zhivako very nervous indeed.

In Moscow the name of Joseph K. was associated with two institutions which he had himself chiefly created. The first of these institutions was known as The Castle. It was to The Castle, thirty kilometres west of the outer suburbs of Moscow, that Joseph K.'s victims were taken to be subjected to the second institution he had created which was known simply as The Trial. Mention of either struck terror into the heart of every Russian bureaucrat still. Joseph K.'s special commission was that of roving investigator assigned to search out weak links in the administration. Joseph K. operated both inside and outside of Moscow. Every year he would spend six months travelling from one embassy to another giving a thorough check to all members of the diplomatic corps. Currently he was in London.

Pyotr Zhivako, third assistant secretary to the ambassador, was a young, handsome Russian with rugged,

Slavic good looks, very blond and with large, candid blue eyes. He had been in London nearly two years and did not want to leave. The main reason he was so nervous in K.'s presence was because he had something to hide — something very important to hide. It was not that he was a traitor — in fact, politically, he was a loyal supporter of the current regime — it was simply that he had a vice that Joseph K. would have disapproved of sufficiently to make him think in terms of The Castle and The Trial. Not that Joseph K. had quite the authority that he had had in the old days — but in a way this made him even more eager to sniff out treachery and revisionism and decadence wherever he could find it, for an institution is no good without a function and Joseph K. needed to keep himself in work in a changing political climate.

Zhivako knew that his secret was well-protected, but nonetheless he was sweating in case Joseph K. should sniff out a clue. If he did that — the investigator would not rest until he had found out the truth.

The garret in which the two men sat overlooked a pleasant flower-garden at the back of a tall, elegant house in Ladbroke Road. The house belonged to the Embassy and currently sheltered the person, family and servants of Fydor Dyescheoffski, Special Attache.

Dyescheoffski was currently the subject of Joseph K.'s investigation. It was simply a routine investigation, but Joseph K. always paid special attention to members of the diplomatic staff who were lodged outside the Embassy.

The reason that Joseph K. and the nervous Pyotr Zhivako sat in the garret room overlooking the flower-garden was because Zhivako had been assigned to introduce Joseph K. to the persons he wished to investigate. K. had just finished his investigation of Dyescheoffski, family and servants and had asked to be lent a room in which he might ponder the information he had been given. He knew from long experience that to closet himself in a room in the house of the people on whom he was checking up usually made them agitated and likely to panic in some way that could reveal some clue to whatever they might be hiding.

Joseph K. had been sitting in silence in the shadows for over half an hour and if the household was not becoming anxious then Pyotr Zhivako certainly was.

He cleared his throat.

"Well, comrade — have you discovered anything suspicious about Comrade Dyescheoffski?" he asked at length.

K. pursed his lips and looked out of his deep-set brooding eyes at Zhivako.

"I am still cogitating, comrade," he said in his stern, distant voice. The voice had been cultivated by K. until it was a splendid instrument in his arsenal for striking terror into the strongest hearts.

"Ah . . . " said Zhivako.

Meanwhile, Jerry Cornell was in a quandary. He had parked his Armstrong-Siddely a mile down the road, close to Shepherd's Bush and was walking cautiously towards Ladbroke Road via the back-doubles. His reason: Maximum secrecy.

The secrecy had nothing to do with the Russians or, indeed, the case he was working on.

The secrecy concerned the very slight chance that Shirley might spot him hanging around in Kensington when he had told her that he would be out of town.

The pleasant tree-lined streets of the area were quiet under the warm, afternoon sun as Cornell, keeping to the shady side of the streets, approached the house in Ladbroke Road and paused to give it the once over.

He didn't relish his assignment.

It could easily result in his discomfort or embarrassment — or (the thought chilled him) even physical violence.

Still, he was stuck. Fry's instructions had been unequivocal.

He had to find out who read *Whoomf!* at the house.

It was Cornell's cowardly nature which, paradoxically, normally got him into his tightest squeezes. The reason for this was that fear turned his mind to jelly and took away his ability to act logically. He would quite often find himself doing the most ludicrous things because his mind was so clouded with terror.

This was what happened now.

Cornell decided that the thing to do was to sneak round to the back of the house and give it a butcher's. There was no logical reason for this. It would have been more sensible to have called at the front door. But sense had deserted the A-Class Agent.

He had noted that there was a large public gardens behind the row of houses. This public gardens backed on to the individual private gardens. There should be little difficulty involved in reaching the back of the house.

The gate to the big gardens was locked, but he managed to climb over it and jump down on to the gravel path beyond. Then he faded into the shrubbery.

Tripping over bits of roots, slapped in the face by swinging branches, he stumbled forward until he reached the fence of the house.

A wonderful scent came from behind it. Peering cautiously over, Cornell saw that the garden was full of beautifully cultivated blooms of all descriptions.

Many were large flowering shrubs and would afford plenty of cover, he decided.

He clambered over the fence and dropped on his belly in the soft soil behind a rhododendron bush.

Inch by inch he began to make his way around the perimeter of the garden towards the house.

Bees buzzed around him in the idyllic garden. They seemed to be laughing at him. But Cornell was too far gone to realise just how ridiculous his plan was. He had somehow managed to confuse the Russians with Shirley in his mind. They were all jumbled up together.

He had no idea what he intended to do when he reached the house.

Probably he would get up and knock on the french windows instead of the front door — and thus add to rather that substract from his embarrassment.

Pyotr Zhivako and the menacing Joseph K. stood by the window of the garret room looking down in some astonishment at the sight of the man crawling through the shrubbery. From this position, high above the garden, they could see everything that went on.

"What do you suppose he's up to comrade?" Zhivako said, glad that K.'s attention had been turned away from thoughts of the staff. "Could he be a burglar?"

"Possibly," Joseph K. agreed in a voice like the winds of limbo, "but in cases of this kind it is always better to suspect that an intruder like that is the agent of an un-friendly power."

"You mean a spy!" Zhivako's eyes lighted up. "After our secrets?" A spy scare of this kind would definitely take the heat off the staff and Zhivako's own secret would be safe.

"I think it likely. Either it is mere coincidence that he should choose today to do whatever he plans to do, or else he has some assignation with a member of this house-hold."

"If the latter were true, comrade," Zhivako said ner-vously, "surely he would approach in some more direct way?"

"You never know with these imperialists," K. told him. "You never know."

The intruder's face had been turned away from them up until now, but then he looked up.

Joseph K. gave a grunt of recognition, then a cold,

mirthless laugh.

"So . . . " he murmured. "So . . . they have put their top man on the job. This must be something bigger than I suspected. Much, much bigger. What luck that I should be here at the moment the Wolf of London decides to pay a call!"

"The — er — 'Wolf of London'?" Zhivako enquired.

"Yes, comrade — though you may know him by other names. He is British Intelligence's most feared agent. He is utterly ruthless, incredibly intelligent, a master of disguise and subterfuge. He speaks most languages fluently. Only recently he single-handedly wiped out a widespread Chinese plot to blow up most of London and personally arrested Kung Fu Tzu."

"Kung Fu Tzu is captured?" Zhivako was astonished.

"Even now the Chinese Master Agent lies in a secret prison — put there by the man you see below us."

"Who is he?" Zhivako asked, wide-eyed. "Who is he, comrade?"

"The ace agent of the British," K. replied. "In Peking he is known as the Wolf of London — in Moscow he is known as The Bloodletter — in Berlin his code-name is Herr Fear — in Prague they call him Steelhand — in Belgrade he is called The Monster — in Warsaw they call him The Destroyer . . . "

K.'s eyes narrowed. Cornell had risen from the ground and was walking towards the french windows.

"Not — not — Cornell . . . " Zhivako whispered. "I hardly believed such a man existed. I thought him an invention of the propaganda department to keep us on our toes. . . "

Again K. laughed chillingly.

"They even have a name for him in the S.I.C. files in the U.S.A."

"Wh-what do they call him there?"

"Superagent!" K. hissed.

Superagent, his suit covered in bits of leaf and lumps of

44

mud, was currently leaning against the wall by the french windows wondering how he got there.

The process was familiar, of course. He had lost his head as usual. Now there was nothing else to do but try to go back the way he had come.

The french windows opened. He turned with a start, an apology on his lips.

At first it seemed there was no-one there. Then he looked down.

Looking up at him was a little boy in a blazer and short flannel trousers. The thing that caught Cornell's eye immediately was the comic he clutched in his hand.

"Who are you?" the little boy said haughtily in a faintly-accented voice.

"Um . . . " said Cornell.

"You the gardener?"

"Er . . . " Cornell recovered himself sufficiently to nod gratefully. "That's right – the gardener. I've been tracing the roots of the crab-apple tree."

"You aren't half mucky," said the little boy.

"It's a mucky job," Cornell said weakly.

The comic the little boy clutched was *Whoomf!* Cornell recognised the familiar pictures of the Devil Rider on the front.

"That your comic?" he asked.

"Of course it is. You can't borrow it. It only just came in the post today . . . "

"You get it by mail, then?"

"None of your business," said the little boy.

"Your name's Dyescheoffski then?"

"What's it to you?"

"You're the subscriber!" Cornell said inanely – and with some relief. "That's why a copy's sent here!" He laughed crazily. "Phew!"

Another red-herring. He was safe.

"Well." He grinned stupidly, dusting down his suit. "I'll

be off, then . . . "

"You haven't been paid," the little boy informed him.

"I'll send in my bill," Cornell told him. He began to saunter back across the lawn towards the flower-beds and the fence beyond.

"Did you trace the roots?"

"Oh — er — yes. I'll send you the plans in the morning."

·Cornell broke into a crazy run, crashed through a thicket of prize dahlias and vaulted the fence.

The little boy shrugged and went out on to the lawn to sit down and read the comic. He always looked forward to *Whoomf!*

Joseph K. watched Cornell disappear. He rubbed his long jaw and then turned his attention to the little boy who now lay on the grass reading his comic.

K. frowned. He thought he knew what Cornell was up to. He probably planned to kidnap the little boy and blackmail his father. It was what he would have had done if he wanted something from his father.

But what did Dyescheoffski *père* have that Cornell wanted?

He laid a cold, clammy hand on Zhivako's arm. "Get after him, Zhivako — see if you can find him. Then follow him. Don't let him out of your sight — and don't let him see you. Cornell has no compunction about wiping out those he even suspects might be his enemies."

"B-but . . . " Zhivako began.

"Hurry — he will doubtless leave the gardens by the gate. You may be able to catch up with him there."

Zhivako left the garret. He was not altogether sure that he was happy that the heat was off him personally. It might be on him again now — in a way that was just as nerve-racking. It simply wasn't fair that he should be told to follow the most feared secret agent in the imperialist world.

46

CHAPTER SEVEN

AS JERRY CORNELL made his way back towards Shepherds Bush where his Armstrong-Siddely was parked, he heard the sound of horse's hooves behind him. The sound was familiar enough in this area where dozens of totters plied their trade and Cornell paid it no attention.

It was only when he heard the other sound that he turned to stone and stood stock still.

"Ker, ker, ker, ker . . . " went the other sound. "Ker, ker, ker, kaaarrrraaaaheeer . . . "

Cornell turned slowly, pale-faced.

The totter, driving an incredibly decrepit horse, towing an even more decrepit cart was twice as decrepit as either.

"'Ullo, Jerry," said the totter. "Ker, ker, ker . . . "

"Uncle Edmond," Cornell whispered. "What are you doing here?"

"Watcher think — doin' me — ker, ker, ker — rounds, in' I?" Uncle Edmond was just one member of Cornell's embarrassing family. Uncle Edmond deserved the name by which he was known from the Bush to the Dale. The name was Tatty Ted. He was famous for his filthiness and his horrible cough. That was the other sound Jerry had recognised.

Clad in miscellaneous rags that had only their incredible dirtiness in common, Uncle Edmond sat hunched on the seat of his smelly cart, a collection of rusting metal and rotting furniture in the back.

"Well, I must be off," said Cornell briskly.

"'Ere, Jerry — carn't I give yer a lift?" Uncle Edmond asked in a wheedling voice.

"No, thanks." Jerry knew that there was only one reason

47

Uncle Edmond would ask and that was because he wanted something. All the Cornell's — and there were scores of them in Notting Hill — wanted something. Jerry Cornell was the only Cornell with money and he was very popular with the family for this reason. Tatty Ted was after a handout and his nephew was not ready to fork out.

"'Ere — you couldn't lend us a coupla quid . . . ?"

Jerry began to walk hurriedly away, but the totter followed him, the horse and cart creaking and squealing as it moved reluctantly along.

"Jerry — 'ang on a minute . . . "

Jerry began to run.

The totter's cart picked up speed and began to chase Cornell down the long, tree-lined street.

Gradually, it began to overtake the running man.

"Jerry!" cried Uncle Edmond. "Ker-ker-ker — Jerry!"

Now the horse began to echo Uncle Edmond's cough as it exerted itself too much. Clattering, coughing and yelling the terrible manifestation pursued him until he could run no more.

Beaten, he turned.

As he did so, he saw a figure dart suddenly into the entrance of a house. He recognised the signs at once. He was being followed — perhaps by Shirley or someone Shirley had put on to him.

Uncle Edmond was looking down at him sorrowfully.

"Sorry ter bovver yer, Jerry — since yer innan 'urry, ker-ker-ker — but . . . "

The damp eyes (seemingly filled with stagnant water) regarded Jerry pleadingly.

Cornell came to a decision.

"I will take that lift, Uncle Edmond. Thanks." Suppressing his disgust, he climbed up on to the seat beside his filthy uncle.

"Abart the two quid . . . " Uncle Edmond began.

"Get moving," Cornell told him. "We'll discuss it later.

Go as fast as you can."

The cart lurched forward, almost precipitating Jerry into the rubbish at the back.

Behind him, Zhivako began to trot along in pursuit of the cart. This man Cornell was reputed to have a network of helpers throughout London. It seemed to be true. Half-expecting the cart to turn into a streamlined helicopter, Zhivako doggedly continued to trail it.

Cornell glanced back once.

Zhivako couldn't see his expression, but he knew Cornell had spotted him.

He knew then that he was a marked man.

However things worked out in the duel of wits between Cornell and Joseph K., Zhivako felt he would be a lucky man indeed if he were to come out of this encounter in one piece.

When Uncle Edmond took him to the street in which he'd left the Armstrong-Siddely, Cornell paid him the couple of quid, dropped from the cart and sprinted for the car.

The engine was slow in starting. The battery needed re-charging and it took a while before the engine coughed into life. Through the rear-view mirror, Cornell could see the man who had followed him skulking behind a telegraph pole further up the street. He wondered if it were a private detective Shirley permanently hired to keep an eye on him. That might explain Shirley's uncanny ability to find his latest girl friend every time and frighten her off. Why hadn't he thought of that in the first place?

As he drove away, he saw the private detective desperately trying to flag down a taxi without success. He smiled thinly. He'd given the man the slip. He'd have to think up some story to give Shirley, but that didn't seem so important now.

He glanced at his watch.

Time to phone the office from a pub in Fleet Street,

have a quick one, and then meet the delicious Judy Judd in the Black Swan.

He'd tell Fry that the lead on the embassy official was a blank and that he felt his own line of enquiry — finding out who wrote the Devil Rider strip — was a better one. He could tell Fry that Judy Judd was his contact and that would cover him for tonight. He was looking forward to tonight.

CHAPTER EIGHT

PYOTR ZHIVAKO HAD failed. Joseph K. had given him a job to do and he had fallen down on it.

Now Joseph K. paced up and down in the garret room. Occasionally he would turn and glare at the quaking young Russian.

Zhivako had returned to discover that Joseph K. had put the Dyescheoffski family under house arrest for their own safety. It would make Cornell's task more difficult if he still intended kidnapping the child. Cross-examining the boy, Joseph K. had discovered that Cornell had made some mysterious reference to plans before he had left. To his knowledge none of the Dyescheoffskis had any plans that Cornell might want. It was just possible that Dyescheoffski was a traitor, of course. That line of enquiry must be thoroughly examined. In the meantime Joseph K. wanted to know Cornell's movements. Somehow he must find Cornell again.

He snapped his fingers abstractedly.

The sound startled Zhivako and he looked questioningly at Joseph K., but the investigator was not paying attention to him.

"What do you want me to do, comrade?" Zhivako asked eventually.

"You seem incapable of performing the simplest tasks . . ." K. replied acidly. "I see nothing for you to do . . . "

"I wasn't trained in espionage, comrade . . . " Zhivako said lamely.

"You were trained in loyalty to your nation — that should have been enough. You young men are all soft. No

51

one is reliable any more."

"I'm sorry, comrade . . . "

K. snapped his fingers again.

"Get out!" he said. "Go away. I must think."

Zhivako scuttled from the room gratefully. With luck Joseph K. would not bother to use him again and, now that the investigator's attention was on larger matters, the question of Zhivako's particular vice being discovered was no longer particularly worrying.

On his way downstairs he passed little Evgeni Dyescheoffski, still clutching his copy of *Whoomf!*

"Why can't we leave the house?" the boy asked.

"For your own safety," Zhivako said importantly.

In the hall Fydor Dyescheoffski and his fat wife stood looking anxious. Fydor was a man of middle years with a shock of spiky brown hair and a round, flat-featured face.

"Hello, comrade," he said. "What's this all about? Am I suspected?"

There was a note of respect and caution in Fydor Dyescheoffski's voice. Previously he had always spoken somewhat patronisingly to Zhivako. The young man felt embarrassed.

"We shall see," he muttered mysteriously as he pushed past them and left the house.

The craving was on him — doubtless sparked off by his encounter with Joseph K.

The craving, once it came, had to be satisfied. It didn't matter what danger there was of discovery, what ignominy he might suffer, what degradation he might be forced to — the need had to be fed.

Dry-lipped, the young Russian hurried back towards the hostel where, hidden under the floorboards, he kept the tools of his vice.

Jerry Cornell helped Judy Judd from his car which he had to park some distance away from The Secretary

Bird pop-club.

She gave him a big smile and took his arm as they walked towards Wardour Street through the crowds who thronged Soho's pavements.

At the door a huge man — plainly an ex-boxer — blocked their path. Then he recognised Judy Judd and beamed.

"Evening, Miss Judd."

"Evening, Mr Drummond," she replied.

They went down some steps and entered a basement where their way was blocked again — this time by a counter at which sat another huge man. He could have been Mr Drummond's brother.

He nodded to Judy and opened the flap to let them pass through.

The noise was incredible. It throbbed and sobbed and pounded in the murky room which they entered. A few couples were on the floor dancing. Elsewhere, around the walls and sitting on the few seats in front of the stage, others stood simply looking about them rather boredly. The place was fairly large, but very dimly lighted. On their left was a Coca Cola bar and further ahead, on the left of the stage was a stall that seemed to sell coffee and hot dogs. There was no one on stage. The music came from loudspeakers on various parts of the walls.

There was a very seedy atmosphere in The Secretary Bird club. Cornell felt immediately at home.

They went to the bar and had a Coca Cola each. Cornell winced at the price he was charged. The club was beginning to fill up now. Surprisingly, only so many were teenagers. Most of the clients — men, at least — seemed to be in their middle twenties. The girls were on the whole younger in fantastic get-ups. The baroque dress of the girls contrasted oddly with the in general fairly conservative clothes of the men though there was a fair smattering of modish males. There were also many West Indians, mainly men.

After about half an hour, in which it was impossible to talk, Cornell saw the musicians begin to come on stage. There was an organist, two saxophonists, a drummer, a guitarist and a bass guitarist. They were dressed in clothes even further out that those of the people on the floor. The organist wore a fur deerstalker, an opera-cape, a T-shirt with the slogan 'Jesus Saves' on it, riding boots and a pair of red, white and blue underpants. The rest of the players were dressed in equally bizarre costume.

A few people clapped, but most of the audience pretended to ignore the performers.

The band began to play.

If the noise of the records had been loud, the noise of the band — for all that the music was surprisingly excellent — was ear-shattering. Huge amplifiers, turned up at full volume, seemed almost to bounce from their supports as The Wilful Mad gave a standard 'I Go Crazy' all they had.

"If you leave me, I'll go crazy . . . " sang the bass player, his long legs pumping up and down in time to his beat.

More people were dancing now and Cornell saw that, in the absence of a chance to chat-up a girl, the men would simply grab someone and hope for the best. Sometimes they were rejected with a slap in the face (which they accepted cheerfully) but most of the time the girls would blank their faces and begin to frug.

Judy pulled Jerry on to the dance floor. He had no idea how one frugged, but he jerked about in front of her and she seemed to be having a good time, her huge breasts bouncing along in time to the music.

The first number over, the band went straight into the second, a slower song called "Bring it on home to me."

Jerry grabbed Judy, pulled her to him and, chest to chest, began to swing round the dance floor.

"Oh, how *camp*!" She shouted in delight above the music. "How perfectly George Raft!"

She was referring to his foxtrot.

CHAPTER NINE

STIFF-LEGGED JERRY CORNELL walked towards the
bar to get Judy Judd and himself a coke. Foxtrotting or
jiving — or even imitation-frugging — certainly took it out
of you, he thought. He'd caused quite a stir in The Secretary
Bird with his jive. He was so behind he was far-out.

As he paid for the drinks Cornell glanced casually around
the dimly lit place.

Suddenly he saw the private detective who had trailed
him earlier that day. The man was in full fab gear. He had
a military-style jacket, bell-bottom hipsters, a lemon-
yellow shirt with a wide floral tie and square-toed patent-
leather boots. Since he was in his early thirties, the clothes
looked just a trifle odd on him, but he wore them with
some dash.

Was it coincidence, Cornell wondered, or had the man
managed to trail him to the club?

The private detective had grabbed hold of a girl in a
skirt so short its hem was above the line of her pants.
He seemed engrossed in the girl and the music. His eyes
had a glassy look about them, his movements as he danced
were ritualistic, ecstatic.

Jerry tapped his fingers on the bar and wondered what
to do. If the private detective spotted him, then he would
doubtless call Shirley who would doubtless trace Judy who
would doubtless be scared off like the others.

Cornell decided to leave.

He went to look for Judy.

Judy was dancing with a seven-foot negro in a Frank
Sinatra hat and sagger-boy trousers. The man's face wore
a wide smile as Judy postured in front of him and he

postured in turn. Cornell felt jealous.

He tried to catch Judy's attention. But she was Gone. He would have to wait till the number ended.

As the number ended, Pyotr Zhivako drew the girl to him and began to kiss her passionately on the mouth. His eyes were closed for some time, but, as he opened them (still kissing the nameless girl) he saw someone he recognised across the room. The man was tapping a tall redhead on the shoulder. The redhead was looking into the eyes of a huge negro. Neither redhead nor negro interested Pyotr Zhivako — the other man interested him very much.

Zhivako started violently and the girl bit his tongue. He yelped and staggered back.

"Are you barmy?" the girl asked casually, putting her head on one side and looking at him clinically.

"Ah!" Zhivako said by way of reply and began to back towards the door of the club.

The man he had seen was Cornell the Master Agent — Cornell the Bloodletter — the man they called in Berlin *Mr. Fear*!

Cornell must have come here looking for him. Zhivako knew that Cornell would guess his vice immediately and that would give the agent a hold over Zhivako.

Zhivako's secret vice was, of course, fab clothes and pop music — both more than frowned upon by the establishment. Should anyone at the embassy find out, Zhivako would be shipped home immediately. And at home — whatever happened to him — he would no longer be able to wear his fab gear and attend his pop clubs. Withdrawal symptoms would set in almost immediately. He would be completely insane within three months.

Zhivako shuddered at the thought.

The door seemed so far away.

The girl looked in increasing astonishment at Zhivako's peculiar antics.

They were only equalled — thought she couldn't see them — by the peculiar antics of the man in old-fashioned clothes who was currently shaking a young redheaded women by the shoulder.

Judy Judd seemed in a temporary state of trance.

Cornell muttered into her op-earringed ear.

"Judy! Wake up, Judy. We've got to leave."

Judy didn't hear him.

Cornell glanced behind him and saw the private detective backing warily towards the door. The detective had seen him and was doubtless on his way to phone Shirley.

Cornell's mouth was dry.

"Judy!"

The negro smiled at Cornell. He pointed at his large gleaming eyes.

"Ah've got her, mon — with mah ahyes hyah," said the West Indian. "Raas, mon!"

Cornell tried to ignore him and shook Judy even more roughly.

Gradually the dazed expression left Judy's face. The negro looked upset and tried to fix her with his eyes again, but he was unsuccessful.

Judy turned to look at Cornell.

"Hell, Jerry," she said, "that was lovely. For a moment I thought you were a big, seven-foot . . . "

She saw the West Indian, who had walked away in disappointment, and her voice trailed off. "Oh . . . "

"We've got to leave," Cornell said desperately.

"My place?" Judy suggested sweetly.

"That would be nice," Cornell agreed with alacrity. He began to feel relieved. Things were working out all right again.

The Wilful Mad were leaving the stage, their first set completed.

As Cornell guided Judy towards the door he saw the private detective disappear rapidly up the steps of the club.

Cornell congratulated himself that by the time the man got to the phone he and Judy would be well on their way to Judy's flat.

But as they reached the steps he looked up and saw a familiar leg.

He knew the leg very well indeed. He knew it by sight and he knew it by texture.

It was the leg of his wife.

It was, in a word, Shirley's leg.

Shirley's hips, swinging meaningfully, appeared, then Shirley's breasts and neck.

At the sight of Shirley's grim, set face — lovely but terrifying — Cornell gave a slight moan and tried to scramble back into the club.

She must have been waiting outside. She must have come with the private detective.

Cornell pushed Judy away from him and tried to smile. Shirley smiled in return.

It was the smile of a goddess of ice.

Judy frowned.

"What did you do that for, Jerry?" she said.

"Jerry? I'm not Jerry," said the desperate Cornell. "At least — yes — I'm Jerry. Who are you?"

"Not good enough." Shirley's voice, cool and firm, cut through the fug of the club.

"Who are you?" Judy said, putting her hands on her hips and letting her hypnotic earrings swing menacingly.

"The Wife," said Shirley, advancing.

"Here, Shirley — this isn't what you think," Cornell said. "It's the case — she's my contact."

"I think you've had enough contact already." Shirley pushed past her husband and took Judy Judd's arm.

"Let go of me!" Judy cried.

Shirley ignored her and propelled her towards the ladies' lavatory nearby.

Cornell watched them disappear inside.

58

He seemed paralysed, unable to move a muscle as he waited, his eyes fixed on the entrance of the lavatory.

Time passed. How much, he could not tell.

At length Judy emerged.

Her face was pale. She avoided Jerry's questioning glance. Her lips were moving feebly. There was a slight, but obvious, nervous tic on the left side of her face. She walked mechanically, arms limp at her sides, back into the club.

Shirley came out a few moments later.

She dusted her hands.

"Wha — ?" began Jerry.

Shirley gave him a warm smile. It froze Jerry's blood.

"We won't have any more trouble from her," Shirley said, walking towards the steps.

"Wha — ?" Jerry said again.

"Don't thank me," she said. "I know how hard it is not to get emotionally involved in a case — but I've cleared all that away now. Keep going, Jerry. Good luck."

The ice goddess ascended.

Jerry felt funny all over.

After a while he managed to totter back into the club. He saw Judy in a corner with the negro. He started to approach her, but then thought better of it. He wondered just what Shirley had said to Judy. Whatever it was, it must have been the same thing she said to all his girl-friends. He knew there wasn't much point in approaching Judy. It would only unnerve him to see the wild look come into her beautiful face and listen to the little moaning sounds she would make.

Despairingly he went and sat down in one of the seats near the stage.

After a while the band came back and began to play. Lost in a sea of sound, Cornell sat there in a daze.

Next to him a soft arm, clad in a light silk jacket of

pastel paisley, moved slightly in time to the music.

He hardly noticed it.

For the moment, at least, his interest in women was gone.

His main object in life was now to stay away from Shirley for a while. There was something definitely occult in the way she managed to find his girl-friends almost as soon as he had met them. There was something that smacked of black magic in the way she managed to scare them off once she had found them.

The beat was 4/4, but Jerry trembled in 7/8.

In the Leicester Square public lavatory, Jerry Cornell's private detective — actually the depraved Zhivako — was hastily ridding himself of his fab clothes and transferring them to a case in which he kept his brown serge suit.

For the moment the craving was over. He could last at least a couple of days without having to satisfy it.

Sight of the abominable Cornell had put the fear of Lenin into him. There was, perhaps, one way in which he could make capital of the encounter. If he phoned Joseph K. and told him he had seen Cornell enter the club, it might lose him K.'s disapproval and take the heat off him altogether.

He hurried from the lavatory bearing his suitcase, deposited it in the left luggage locker in Leicester Square Tube Station and searched for the nearest phone.

He found it and began to dial the number of Dyescheoff-ski's house where Joseph K. had permanently billeted himself while dealing with the Cornell case.

After an hour of the music, Jerry became a little more settled. He was becoming increasingly aware of the soft arm that touched his. Even when he moved away the arm seemed to creep up to his and touch him again.

Gradually he turned his head.

The blonde who sat beside him was, in his own terms,

stunning.

She had very long, fine platinum blonde hair, a tall, graceful figure. Her longish face was perhaps the most beautiful Cornell had ever seen. It bore hardly any make-up.

The trouser suit she wore, of pastel-green paisley, clung to her wonderful legs and emphasised her high-breasted figure.

On her long fingers she wore large, chunky rings.

Cornell forgot all about Judy Judd and, incredibly, all about Shirley.

He fell in love with the girl beside him.

She turned her face of transcendental beauty towards him and winked.

"Oh!" said Cornell.

"Hello," said the large, yearning lips.

"Oh!"

Only once before had Cornell felt this way about a woman. And she had been a very different woman indeed. She had enslaved him utterly. Her name had been Lilli von Bern — the legendary female spy.* This girl was much younger than Lilli — possibly just twenty-one. She had the face of an angel — all sweetness and promise — whereas Lilli had been something different altogether.

"Oh!"

"Do you want to dance with me?" asked the angel.

"Yes . . . " Cornell whispered. "Oh, yes . . . "

They got up and went on to the floor. He took the soft figure to him. He felt her body through the folds of the thin, silk trouser suit. She moved against him as no girl had ever moved before.

When they had danced for some time, the music stopped.

"What's your name?" asked the vision.

"Jerry — Jerry Cornell."

"A lovely name."

"What's yours?"

"Polly," she said. "Polly Snapgirdle."

*See THE CHINESE AGENT

"I love you," said Jerry.

"You're wonderful," said Polly Snapgirdle.

"Your name is lovely, too."

"Get away," said the vision.

"It is, it is!" Jerry said with heartfelt sincerity.

That's what love does to a man.

The club's evening session was over. It was just past eleven o'clock.

Through the littered, seedy room two people wandered hand in hand.

Jerry Cornell's face was radiant as he stared into the beautiful face of his love.

Polly Snapgirdle stared deep into his eyes and smiled her sweet, sweet smile.

Oblivious of everything but each other, the lovers trod on air, swept across the floor and went up the steps to the crowded street.

"Oh, Polly," Jerry Cornell said. "I'm so happy."

"I'm happy too, Jerry," she said softly.

"Oh, Polly — what shall we do now?"

"Anything you want to, Jerry. Anything . . . "

"Oh, Polly . . . "

As if in a dream he took her to his car. She gave him her address.

The Armstrong-Siddely — a magic coach — bore them through the neon-jewelled streets towards Chelsea, where Polly Snapgirdle lived.

No thought of Shirley intruded on Jerry Cornell's bliss. Besides, it was obvious that having scared one girl off she would not expect him to find another so quickly.

Cornell sighed and took Polly Snapgirdle in his free arm.

Following behind, in a taxi, came two men.

One was the bulky Joseph K., his hands clenched over the handle of a thick, hawthorn walking stick. Beside him, almost as bulky in his brown serge suit, sat Pyotr Zhivako, wishing that Joseph K. hadn't thought it necessary for him to come along.

"We will watch him, only," K. said to the young Russian. "We will study his movements. Then, when the right time presents itself, we will pounce — and we will kill swiftly. It is the only way to deal with someone of this Cornell's powers."

Pyotr Zhivako didn't feel much up to pouncing on anyone at the moment — least of all the almost-mythical Cornell, conqueror of Kung Fu Tzu and a host of other agents.

CHAPTER TEN

CORNELL WOKE RELAXED and happy.

He looked dreamily up into the canopy of Polly Snap-girdle's fourposter.

There was no doubt about it. The place had a quality of its own — a quality that fitted the character of his princess.

He turned his head and looked at his princess as she lay there with her blonde hair spread on the pillow, a sweet smile on her sleeping face. A bare, creamy shoulder peeped over the apricot sheet.

He sighed with delight.

Slowly Polly's great, luminous eyes opened.

"Hello — Jerry," she said with the barest possible hesitation.

"Hello, darling," Jerry said adoringly. "Hello, Polly . . ."

"Hello."

"Hello . . . "

Polly smiled at him sweetly.

"What time is it?"

Jerry looked at his watch.

"Eleven o'clock, Polly darling . . . "

"Darling . . . "

"Polly . . . "

"Hello, Jerry."

"Hello, Polly. It's good to see you . . . " He paused as reality impinged.

Eleven o'clock.

"Christ," he said to his vision. "I'll have to have a good story for Fry. Any chance of some breakfast?"

The vision's face looked troubled.

Obviously girls like Polly didn't expect to leap out of

bed and start frying eggs. For a moment Jerry missed the obliging Shirley's three-course breakfasts.

"Can I use the phone?" he said.

"Of course, darling," said Polly and buried her face in the apricot-frilled pillow.

Jerry climbed out of the vast bed, crossed the silk carpet, sat down naked in the gold chair by the rococco phone and sneaked a look back over his shoulder. Polly appeared to have gone back to sleep.

He dialled the number of the office.

"Hello, Jerry," said Fry, his voice sounding faintly disturbed. "Has the contact given you anything concrete yet?"

"Nothing exactly concrete, sir . . . "

"You haven't found out who's writing the Devil Rider script?"

"Sorry, sir, not yet."

"You sound tired, Jerry? Had a rough time? What happened?"

"Can't talk over the phone, sir. I'll be in touch as soon as I can . . . "

Fry paused.

"Who was your contact?" he said at length.

"A girl, sir."

"Not a redhead called Judd?"

"Yes, sir."

"Then you'd better look for a new one, Jerry." Fry's voice was embarrassed.

"Why, sir?"

"Get over to the Wayflete Building if you can. You'll find out." Fry replaced the receiver.

Cornell cursed. What had happened at the Wayflete Building? There was no way out of it. He'd have to go there and see for himself — if only to cover himself for the time spent with Polly.

He made a mental note of Polly's phone number and

picked his clothes up from the floor. Polly didn't stir in her ripe, sybaritic bed as he pulled on his clothes and left. As long as he didn't look at her face he was okay. In that respect Polly Snapgirdle resembled the Medusa. She could turn him to stone easy as looking at him.

CHAPTER ELEVEN

HE PULLED UP the Armstrong-Siddely outside the Way-flete Building, careless of the double yellow line.

He ran up the steps of the building and waited impatiently for the lift.

It came at last.

He jumped in and went up to the ninth floor.

The corridor was crammed with depraved office boys, seedy staff journalists and white-coated tea-ladies (who were probably somebody's mother and made Cornell feel sorry for whoever's they were). They were talking in a kind of hushed babble.

Cornell pushed through the throng. He hardened his face and looked vital to the case (a trick he had mastered in the course of his misspent life picking up unconsidered trifles in the moments following the crisis). He didn't know if there were a case, but it got him through the crowd.

A respectful ring stood around the door of an office marked 991. Underneath were the words TEEN SCREAM: Judy Judd, Editor.

He murmured something firm and opened the office door.

It was a large office, painted in dirty white. On the window sill stood two pots containing drooping African violets. Pop stars hung on every available part of every wall. A big hi-fi set stood in one corner, piled high with 45s and LPs. Opposite it was a big desk.

There was a lot of blood about, particularly on the desk, and the wood and surrounding walls were charred.

On the floor were the twisted, blackened remains of an Imperial 5060 typewriter. Hanging on the ruined carriage-return lever was a crumpled Donovan cap.

A man came out of a door in the left wall. He wore

overalls. He advanced towards the remains of the type-writer, saw Cornell and turned.

"Are you here on business, sir?"

"What happened?" Cornell asked predictably.

"If you're not on business . . . " the man began.

A burly figure appeared in the doorway, Cornell recognised the bucolic face, the bowler hat, the heavy overcoat, the pipe. All belonged to an acquaintance.

"Aha," said the acquaintance. "Oho!"

It was Detective Inspector Arthur Crapper, bastion of the force, righter of wrongs, guardian of the populace.

"Ho!" said Cornell *"HO!"*

"Ho, ho, ho," gerrumphed the Detective Inspector.

"What the hell are you doing here?" asked Cornell, tiring of this interplay.

"Murder," pronounced the Det. Insp. heavily. "Premediated bloody murder, Mr. Cornell. And might I ask what you're doing here?"

"Government business," Cornell replied briskly. "Is Miss Judd all right?"

"Not for me to say," said Crapper looking piously up at the ceiling and regretfully down at the floor. "Depends which way she went."

"She's not dead?"

"Very much dead. Blown up — with a typewriter. Dirty business, Mr Cornell. One of the worst I've come across. We've established that it was the letter B that did the trick."

"Trick?"

"Blew her up. The typewriter was wired to a tiny but lethal bomb — plastic explosive of some kind. When she pressed the letter B — BAM!"

Offended by Crapper's native vulgarity, Cornell turned away. A tear coursed down one cheek.

It was not a tear of regret. It was not a tear of pity.

It was a tear of despair. Somehow he had got himself entangled in an actual case.

CHAPTER TWELVE

CORNELL DECIDED THAT it was high time he left before anyone saw him.

He murmured something to Crapper and retreated to the door, opened it and closed it hastily behind him. He assumed his official air and began to push his way back through the crowd with the expression of a man who is needed elsewhere.

"Any news?" said a small, spectacled man, with the face of a bewildered rabbit.

"Can't say anything now," Cornell said, as the crowd drew back to let him pass.

But the rabbity man was following him. He speeded up and ran towards the lifts.

When he reached the lift he had to wait for a moment.

It went down slowly, the way lifts sometimes do (as if possessed of wills of their own), stopping at every floor.

When he got down the rabbity man was waiting for him. He was puffing a little. He had evidently run downstairs all the way.

"Here!" he whispered. "I can tell you something."

Cornell started to push by him.

"Sorry, chum, I'm in a hurry."

"Something about the murder," said the rabbity man enticingly.

Cornell shuddered. "Keep it to yourself — I mean, tell the police."

The small man caught him by the cloth of his jacket. Cornell, with an unpleasant grimace, shrugged him off. He gave the man a bitter look. "Do you mind?" he said.

The small man seemed upset. "I said I had information," he protested.

"Tell Scotland Yard," Cornell said savagely, and walked out into the street.

In Great Pie Street the little man grabbed him again. "I've got to tell you. I know who done it and why. Let's go somewhere quick or I'll get it the way Judy did if they see me and you together."

Horrified, Cornell put two and two together and branded the man Jonah.

If he knew anything, he meant trouble for Cornell, and Cornell would have run a mile barefoot over hotcoals to avoid that kind of trouble — or, indeed, any kind.

"Meet me in the Falstaff at twelve-thirty," he said, thinking fast. "Got that?"

"I'll be there," said the rabbity man. He vanished.

Cornell straightened his jacket, looked nervously up and down busy Great Pie Street, and got into the Armstrong-Siddely.

He was off in a flash.

A little while later two men — one in black, one in brown — hurried along the pavement waving a taxi. The one in black was Joseph K. The one in brown was Zhivako.

They had been on Cornell's trail since the night before. They did not want to lose him now.

At least, Joseph K. didn't want to lose him.

Pyotr Zhivako very much wanted to lose him, but had no choice.

Cornell stopped the car in a side road and hurried into the Red Lion in Red Lion Court.

Four or five large gins later he began to feel more his usual self (his usual self usually had at least four or five large gins in him).

He was wondering desperately how he was going to justify leaving the scene of the crime so fast. He'd have to concoct some story about having seen someone making off. It would just about do.

He decided to drive to somewhere like Hackney and phone the office from there. Then he'd hang around for a while and come back, saying he'd lost his man.

Feeling better, Cornell walked towards the exit.

He walked straight into Det. Insp. Arthur Crapper.

"Hullo, hullo," said the Det. Inst., sucking on his pipe.

"Hello," said Cornell wearily. "What's the time?"

Arthur Crapper glanced at his watch and said "One o'clock," automatically. Then he frowned and cast an offensive eye over Cornell's collar-brushing hair, stubble and faintly dirty shirt.

Crapper allowed a look of distaste to pass over his face.

"Well, well," he said heavily. "Why did you rush away like that? I thought your people were interested in the case — you didn't seem interested enough to stay and hear about it . . . "

Cornell had a sneaking suspicion that Crapper had him taped better than most people.

"Don't put it like that, inspector," he said. "You'll be warning me officially next."

"I wouldn't mind," Crapper said reflectively. "You must have been the last to see him alive."

"Her, you mean," Cornell corrected him.

"Her, too, I suppose – you mean the woman, Judy Judd. But I meant Henry Fairbright."

"Who?"

"Henry Fairbright. He was an accounts clerk at Wayflete Publications. He was seen talking to you last, wasn't he?"

"He's dead?" Cornell said. "The little chap with glasses?"

"That's the little chap I mean." Crapper sucked on his pipe, staring at Cornell with narrowed eyes. "You seem to be unlucky company for some people, Mr Cornell.

"Maybe they're unlucky company for me . . . " Cornell mused, half to himself.

"What's that?"

"Nothing."

"People saw you two talking on the steps outside Wayflete about ten minutes before he was killed. I'd like to know what it was all about."

Cornell goosepimples began to rise. His yellow streak tingled.

"I wouldn't," he said. "I hope I never do."

"Eh?"

"How can I help you, Inspector?" Cornell said. "Maybe I need protection. Possibly you should lock me up as a chief suspect, eh?"

"None of your sarcasm, Mr Cornell. You didn't have to look at the mess . . . "

"Mess . . . ?" Cornell said weakly, his throat filling with bile.

"I'm not keen on messy murders. Know how this one was done?"

"N-no . . . " Cornell muttered, not wanting to.

"Very hasty job I should think. Very horrible. You know those spikes they use in editorial offices to put discarded papers on — like a bill-spike they are?"

"N-no n-need to f-finish . . . " Cornell told him, but Crapper had got in his stride.

"Someone grabbed him and rammed him down on one — got him in the brain, right through the left eyeball."

"Yeccchh . . . " said Cornell, making for the gents.

"You'd better look out yourself," the Det. Insp. said with satisfaction. "The big saw's coming nearer and nearer to Vera, eh, Mr Cornell?"

"Shut up!" said Cornell in insane panic. He rushed through the door of the gents, leaving behind him a triumphant Det. Insp. Crapper.

As Arthur Crapper turned to the bar, a face popped round the entrance of the saloon bar and disappeared again. It was the face of Pyotr Zhivako. The faithful hound had picked up the scent again.

In the proletarian public bar, he and Joseph K. conferred in a murmur.

"We must liquidate him as soon as possible," K. decided.

CHAPTER THIRTEEN

THE PRESENCE OF extreme danger very rarely sharpened Jerry Cornell's brain.

On the contrary, it rather tended to dull it. In short — the presence of extreme danger turned Jerry Cornell's brain to jelly.

He was on the run.

There was no doubt about it in his mind.

He was in danger from an unknown enemy. He was next on the list if ever a man was next on the list.

He drove the Armstrong-Siddely to Croydon in just over half an hour. There was no need for him to go to Croydon. He wasn't even sure where Croydon was. The action was a blind reflex.

By the time he reached Croydon and parked in a side street he felt just a little calmer. Not much, but a little. He had to think of two kinds of survival. He had to protect his life — that was the chief consideration. He also had to protect his reputation if that were possible.

He had to go to earth and it had to seem to Fry that he was heavily involved in tracking down the spies and killers who were somehow managing to get the secrets out of the Ministry of Defence.

He had to make two phone calls.

The first must be to Fry. It must be cryptic. It must sound desperate (that part wouldn't be difficult) and it would have to be reasonable.

The second would be to Shirley to tell her not to worry and to impress her that he was in very real danger. That way, too, he might get the private detective off his back.

Automatically he glanced into his rear-view mirror. A

taxi had drawn up about a hundred yards behind him.

A head poked out of the window.

Cornell recognised the private detective.

The man's presence was almost a comfort.

Inside the taxi, unseen by Cornell, Joseph K. rubbed his dark jowl thoughtfully. Doubtless Cornell had come out to Surrey to meet a contact. With luck they would be able to see who it was. Either it would be another agent — or possibly even some official from the embassy.

No wonder Cornell was called The Fox in Bucharest.

From the shadows of the cab he watched as Cornell crossed the road and entered a call-box.

Cornell's voice was a dry rasp. He found it difficult to form the words and sound them. Fear did it — but Fry didn't know that. It added authenticity to Cornell's story.

"I think I'm on to something really big, chief," he managed to say.

"You sound in bad trouble, Jerry. Where are you?"

There was no point in lying. "Croydon," Cornell told him. "I — I can't say any more, chief. I'll phone as soon as I can."

"Can't I send some help, man? Don't try to handle it alone if it's too big for you!"

Inspiration momentarily came back to Jerry. "No, chief," he said, "this is my case. I swore to get the people who did that thing to Thorpe — and I will."

"Don't do anything foolhardy, Jerry," said Fry with a note of respect in his voice.

"I'll do what I have to do," Cornell said thickly. "I'll be in touch."

"Good luck, Jerry," Fry told him.

Cornell rang off.

He felt satisfied that he was covered very thoroughly at that end. Shirley would be more difficult. She would believe he was on a case — but she might not believe it didn't involve another woman.

He dialled Shirley's number and inserted his threepence when she picked up the receiver.

"Jerry?"

He breathed heavily into the phone a few times.

"Is that you, Jerry?"

He coughed nastily.

"H-hello, Shirley . . . "

"Jerry! What's going on?"

"I — c-can't t-tell you n-now, Sh-Shirley — I'm in t-trouble. I think I can get out of it, but . . . " He coughed again. He was happy with the sound of his rasping whisper, the tremble in his voice.

"Can I help, Jerry?"

"No — it's something I have to do myself. Listen, Shirley, if anything happens to me . . . "

"Jerry! Don't say that! Tell me what's the matter!" She sounded very worried indeed.

"Someone's trying to kill me," he said after a pause. "And I've got to find them before they find me. It's simple, Shirley — but I can't tell you any more. You understand that."

"Of course — but can't I help?"

"No one can help me in this one," he said. "It's my problem. I'll phone you when I can — but Shirley . . . "

"Yes, Jerry?"

"Don't try to contact me. I mean it — believe me when I say I'm in very real danger."

"I believe you, Jerry." She sounded on the point of tears.

Cornell had achieved his object.

He put the phone down.

The next thing to do was to hare back to Polly Snapgirdle's place and hope he could hide out there for a couple of weeks until the whole business had blown over.

He returned to London at a more leisurely pace.

The taxi followed faithfully behind.

Joseph K. was frowning.

"He must realise that we are on to him," he murmured to the anxious Pyotr Zhivako. "He has warned his contact off. He is a sly one — a cool one — he knows that we are following him and appears not to care."

"What do you think he will do, comrade?" Zhivako asked apprehensively.

"Do?" Joseph K. smiled coldly. "He will do what he has been known to do before, I should think."

"What's that?"

"He will lead us on until he tires of being followed — then he will turn like a wolverine and he will *kill*!"

"Us? Kill us?"

"He will shoot us down in the street. Or he will lure us into some cunning trap. The file in Moscow is full of such exploits performed by this Cornell."

"Then we should stop following him, comrade . . . " Zhivako suggested sensibly.

"No. We will play his game." Joseph K.'s eyes were shining. "We will follow him — but we will time the business carefully. I intend to use his own methods against him. I hope to be able to strike just before he does. I intend to be the wolverine in this encounter. Cornell will be the victim."

Zhivako hoped that K.'s sense of timing was accurate. He was not altogether confident that it was. A cold sweat had begun to break out on his face.

CHAPTER FOURTEEN

THE COLD SWEAT that had become a permanent feature of Jerry Cornell's face had attracted enough grime in its passage through London streets to add to Cornell's normally some-what greasy appearance.

By the time he had crossed Vauxhall Bridge, he decided that he needed a wash. He stopped the car outside the Buckingham Palace Road entrance of Victoria Station and went to the gents for a wash and brush up.

When he came back up the steps, he saw the private detective hanging about near the Left Luggage counter.

Cornell decided that he had better warn him off. Shirley would doubtless do the same, but there was no harm in doing so, too.

He strode towards the private detective.

Zhivako saw Cornell coming and he became paralysed with fear.

Joseph K. had told him to watch this entrance while the special investigator watched the other.

Zhivako was convinced that Cornell had decided to strike like a wolverine.

The young Russian's throat tightened. He dropped the newspaper he had been holding and waited for the end.

Cornell, the Fox of Bucharest, came towards him rapidly. Cornell's face was set in a grim, lethal mask.

Zhivako had not expected Cornell to speak — only to act, but now the master agent opened his mouth.

"You're not needed any more," the master agent said. "Your services aren't required. I know who you are and who you work for. The job's over. Go home."

"Y-you're warning m-me — y-you're g-giving m-me a ch-chance . . . ?" said Zhivako in terrified amazement and relief.

"I'm warning you, yes," Cornell said with a puzzled frown (which to Zhivako looked like a moody, introspective expression as if Cornell found it difficult to understand his own mercy).

"Th-thank you . . . " Zhivako stuttered.

Cornell nodded to him and strode back towards Buckingham Palace Road.

Joseph K. came up in a few seconds. He had seen the encounter.

He looked at Zhivako in astonishment.

"You are alive, comrade?"

"Yes." Zhivako replied, grinning crazily. "Alive! Alive!"

"He is cool, that one!" K. murmured in awed respect. "He must know the game we are playing."

"He — he said he was warning us — that he knew who we were — that we could go home," Zhivako told his boss.

"So — the duel has become one of words as well as wits," said K. with a sardonic, twisted smile. He tapped his hawthorn walking stick against his right leg. "Well, well — Cornell will find me a match for him. I hope."

"Y-you're not taking his warning, comrade?" Zhivako began to tremble.

"Do you think he meant what he said?" K. said. "It was bluff — just a move in the game. Come — we must pursue him!"

They ran back towards their taxi. The driver (a Russian himself and at the service of the embassy) just managed to catch Cornell as he disappeared in the direction of Eaton Square.

When Jerry Cornell arrived outside Polly Snapgirdle's elegant, white-painted late-18th century Chelsea house, he saw that in the place he had parked last night now stood a Mini Cooper of a particularly unpleasant olive green shade.

The mini was parked right outside the elegant front door. Jerry had to park further up the street.

With some alacrity he left the car and made for the door.

He was just about to ring the bell when he saw that the door was on the latch. He pushed it open and entered the luxurious hall.

The hall was carpeted with soft, white Mongolian lamb carpets. There was black rococco iron work everywhere and the walls were also white. There were big mirrors in the hall. Cornell combed his hair and straightened his tie and then ascended the stairs up to the main living room on the first floor.

He knocked lightly on the panelled door and walked in.

Polly was there in a trouser suit of soft, white leather. Her hair was bound casually with a big black Tom Jones bow. She had a heavy tumbler in one hand and lounged in a huge cream armchair. She smiled when she saw Jerry.

"Hello, darling!"

Jerry was looking at Polly's visitor.

The man wore the black jacket and pinstripe trousers of a city gent or a civil servant. He had a tall, distinguished bearing and iron grey hair. His face was finely chiselled and he looked a gent of the old school. He made Cornell feel uncomfortable. The man also held a big whisky glass.

Jerry thought at first that the man was Polly's father and hoped there wouldn't be trouble.

The man was looking a trifle nervously at Polly.

Polly lept up from the chair and drew Jerry towards the man.

"Jerry, darling, this is John Brook-Hopkins — John this is Jerry Cornell. He really admires your work."

Brook-Hopkins smiled pleasantly. "I'm pleased to hear it, Mr Cornell. I think I'm a bit unfashionable these days, in the main."

"Not at all," Cornell said, racking his brains to remember what Brook-Hopkins actually did. He knew the name, but that was all . . . "Besides, what's fashion, after all . . . ?"

"I suppose you're right," Brook-Hopkins agreed. He downed the last of his whisky. "Besides, we poets don't write for the moment, do we?"

A poet! Now Cornell remembered. Brook-Hopkins was one of a dying breed — the civil service poet. Brook-Hopkins had enjoyed some eminence before the war and just after it. He was interested in Victoriana — especially architecture and a line or two of his work came back to Jerry from schooldays.

Jerry opened his mouth and began:

"Walking up Streatham High Road in the early dawn,
"And treading, boy-like, on the dappled lawn,
"I came upon that mighty pile of stone
"That hearty Bob and pensive Bill had known;
"St Leonard's, simple, plain and clean,
"Where many simple-hearted folk have been
"To send their simple prayers aloft . . . "

"Oh, please, no more . . . " said Brook-Hopkins, raising a large hand and glancing down with false modesty. "I'm glad my little verses please you so much."

"Great stuff— the stuff of England." Cornell said, straight-faced. He remembered Brook-Hopkins when the man had been on the Third Programme in the late forties. He had had a strong, simple, healthy approach to poetry. "Does it rhyme?" he used to ask, or 'Does it scan — in the proper way, I mean?'

"Poetry's in a rotten state," Cornell said ingratiatingly. "I mean this so-called poetry they write to go with jazz and so on."

"Couldn't agree more," Brook-Hopkins said warmly. "Well, it's been very pleasant meeting you, Mr Cornell — I hope we meet again."

"It's been an honour," said Jerry. "I always look out for

your work and your reviews in the Sunday papers."

"I'm delighted."

"We could do with some more of your sort of stuff," Cornell continued.

"Tell that to the poetry publishers," Brook-Hopkins said wryly. "They don't agree with you — do they, Polly?" he added, turning towards Polly Snapgirdle who was pouring Jerry a drink.

"Don't worry, John, darling," she said. "They'll recognise you again. I'm doing my best."

"How are you involved?" Cornell asked, somewhat bluntly, dying to know exactly what relationship Polly had with Brook-Hopkins.

"I'm his agent," she said. "I —" She broke off as the poet gave her a warning look. She smiled. "Don't worry, darling — not a word."

Looking slightly rattled, Hopkins glanced at his watch. "Well, I really must get back to the ministry — don't forget what I asked you, Polly."

"Cheerio, John. I won't. I'll push them up as high as I can."

"Goodbye, Mr Cornell." Brook-Hopkins shook Cornell's hand warmly and then left the room.

Cornell remembered that Brook-Hopkins was quite a high-ranking official with the Ministry of Defence. It was funny how his breed of poet got involved with that sort of job in the end. Either a ministry or the Central Office of Information, he reflected.

"You're a literary agent, are you?" he asked Polly as he sat down next to her and began to stroke her hair.

She handed him his drink. "No," she said. "I'm a commercial artist's agent really, but I handle a few things on the side — and John's work is one of them. Let's not talk about business, darling . . . "

Cornell pressed his lips to hers, running his hands over her marvellous body.

85

A little while later they went upstairs and he helped her off with her white leather suit. They got into the four-poster and began to roll about together.

Jerry forgot his fear.

He forgot the case.

He forgot everything except Polly's marvellous face and body and his own need to enjoy both as much as he could.

CHAPTER FIFTEEN

NEXT MORNING JERRY felt much better. He lay beside Polly feeling warm and happy and safe. He was sure no one would think of looking for him here. There was no better place to hide.

He disentangled one arm from the apricot sheet and looked at his watch.

It was eleven o'clock and he didn't have a thing to do.

He thought he'd get some breakfast for Polly.

He lay there for about twenty minutes before getting out of bed and padding downstairs to the kitchen.

Everything was very neat and modern in the kitchen, as well, of course, as being stylish.

He put some coffee in the coffee maker, put some sliced bread in the toaster, found the butter in the wooden dish, found the marmalade in the earthenware marmalade pot, and soon had a trayful of breakfast all ready.

He carried the big tray upstairs and entered the bedroom just as Polly stirred and turned over yawning.

"Oh, Jerry, darling, how *marvellous* of you!"

He smiled proudly.

"Oh, Jerry!"

"Oh, Polly!"

He got in beside her, balancing the tray, and they began to eat.

"Jerry . . . " she began hesitantly after her first bite of toast.

"Yes?"

"Jerry — what do you do? I mean — you must do something because you were upset about the time yesterday and had to make a phone call . . . "

"I'm a secret agent," he said candidly.

She laughed.

"No — really, what do you do?"

"I'm a secret agent. Honestly."

"How *marvellous*!" She widened her eyes.

"It's just a job . . . "

"No, but it's a *marvellous* job. So romantic. I knew you did something romantic."

"Not so romantic when somebody's trying to kill you," Jerry said comfortably, feeling no fear at all now that he was safe with Polly.

"Not really! Oh, how *marvell* — I mean how *awful*!" She took another bite of toast. "Is someone really trying to kill you, Jerry?"

"They've killed twice — they'll kill me next. I know it. That's — er — one of the reasons I came back here — the main one was to see you again, of course."

"How marvellous!"

It didn't seem marvellous to Jerry, but he let it go.

"You're on the run?" she asked in delight. "You're a marked man?"

"That's about the size of it, yes."

"Super! We'll have to think of places you can hide. Did you ever read *Rogue Male* by Geoffrey Household, where this man . . . "

Jerry had read the book. "Yes," he interrupted hastily. "But I don't think digging a hole in the ground is quite my speed."

"But it was a *tremendous* book . . . "

"Things aren't like that in real life," Cornell told her firmly.

"You mean it's more like *The Spy Who Came In From The Cold?*"

"Not like that either," said Cornell mysteriously. He didn't want to tell her what it was really like — like a Whitehall farce more than anything else.

"What are you going to *do*, Jerry?" she asked breathlessly.

"Well, actually, I had thought of hiding out here . . . " he began.

"Will it be safe, do you think?"

"As safe as anywhere," he said sadly.

"Well, you're welcome, of course," she began doubtfully, "But if you really want to hide somewhere *remote*, I think I know where you could."

"Thanks," he said.

He reached down to the floor where his clothes were strewn and fumbled in his pockets for his cigarettes. He found the case.

It was empty.

Panic set in again.

No fags.

"Have you got a ciggy?" he asked Polly.

"I hoped you had," she said. "I ran out in the night."

Cornell sighed, feeling the withdrawal symptoms beginning to seize him.

Cornell shrugged and began to get up. There was nothing else for it, he supposed.

He donned his grubby shirt and pulled on his crumpled suit. He looked seedier than usual as he walked downstairs to the front door.

As he reached for the handle, someone knocked on the door.

Jerry's mouth went dry.

"Who is it?" he said cautiously.

"Postman."

"I've heard that one before," he said. Risking it, he peered through the magic eye on the door. The man outside with the sour face looked like a postman. He had a postman's uniform and a big, flat parcel in his hand. There was a red post office van with its engine running in the street outside.

Cornell opened the door an inch.

The postman pushed the parcel through and was off, running down to the van.

The van disappeared.

Cornell gingerly put the parcel against the wall. It certainly didn't look like a bomb, but you never knew these days, with all the modern inventions there were about.

He peered round the door and began to sidle along the street towards the cigarette machine.

CHAPTER SIXTEEN

PYOTR ZHIVAKO YAWNED hugely and peered blearily from the bushes of the little park opposite Polly Snapgirdle's house. He saw Cornell emerge and shook Joseph K. — who was dozing in the bush beside him — awake.

"Cornell!" hissed Zhivako. "He's leaving the house."

A hard look came into K.'s eyes. With a practised movement, he slipped the big, heavy Luger from his shoulder holster.

"It must be now," said the special investigator decisively.

As Cornell moved along the pavement towards the cigarette machine. Joseph K. moved along also, using the thick bushes as cover.

Cornell reached the cigarette machine and felt in his pocket for some half-crowns.

. He didn't have one.

All he had were florins and sixpences. He sighed miserably. It wasn't turning out to be his day.

A man in uniform was coming along the street towards him. The man looked as if he wore the uniform of the Guards. He was a large private with a miserable expression on his face.

"Excuse me," Cornell began.

The private of the Guards stopped in front of Cornell — — just as Joseph K. pulled the trigger of his Luger.

The shot rang out from the bushes.

The private looked astonished, then delighted; he staggered, reeled, fell to the pavement.

Cornell paralysed with fear, watched with unblinking eyes as he saw someone scuttling off through the bushes. He got the impression of a black overcoat and nothing else.

He gulped.

Climbing into their taxi, Joseph K. and Pyotr Zhivako looked pale.

"The ruthlessness of the man!" K. muttered. "The utter ruthlessness of him. He must have noticed me in the bushes, realised what I meant to do, and put an innocent passerby between him and the shot. What timing!"

"Perhaps we should contact Moscow to send some more help?" Zhivako suggested miserably. "After all — neither of us is a professional the way Cornell is, comrade."

K. let a little smile flicker over his grim features. "Nonsense — we started the game — we must finish it."

Meanwhile the look of delight on the guardsman's face had increased.

He looked up at Cornell.

"Thank you," he said, clutching his wounded shoulder. "Thank you, sir, whoever you are! I'll always be grateful." He began to crawl off down the road.

Cornell stared after him, mystified.

He didn't know that for the last two years the young private had been trying to get himself out of the army. The wound was the excuse he needed to be declared unfit. With luck he would be invalided out.

Cornell leaned against the cigarette machine sweating.

They knew where he was after all.

The people who had killed Judy Judd and Harry Fairbright so ruthlessly were now about to kill him.

Cornell began to whimper.

Recovering all his remaining strength, he began to stagger back towards Polly's house.

When he reached the door he found that he'd locked himself out.

Feebly, he banged on the door.

It seemed an eternity before Polly, in a pale pink and red striped dressing gown, opened the door.

"Jerry — how *awful*!"

Jerry pushed past her into the hall and fell down.

"Someone took a shot at me," he told her from where he lay.

"The people who are trying to kill you?"

"Who else?" he asked in surprise.

"Of course, darling, how perfectly stupid of me. Oh dear, we must get you away from here." She looked down at him, then gathered her dressing gown about her and bent to help him on to his feet. "Are you actually wounded?"

"Well, not actually *wounded*," he said as he rose. "Not wounded – but nearly."

"You poor darling."

"Someone else got it – the bullet that was meant for me."

"The one with your name on it," she breathed delightedly.

"A soldier got it. He didn't seem to mind. Maybe soldiers don't."

"They expect it, darling, in the course of their work."

She paused.

"Jerry?"

"Yes, Polly?"

"Jerry, did you get the fags?"

He looked aggrieved. "Well, no, I didn't – you see . . . "

"I don't blame you, darling, of course, I suppose I'd better get them myself. Wait here."

Her dressing gown flowing about her, she left the house and hurried down the street.

Jerry trembled.

His eye had fallen on the parcel again.

Maybe it was addressed to Polly, but the devious mind that could turn a typewriter into a bomb wouldn't be balked by a little thing like that. He'd be just as ready to blow them both up as not.

Cornell began to back up the stairs, away from the bomb.

CHAPTER SEVENTEEN

POLLY JOINED HIM in the living room five minutes later. She had a packet of cigarettes in one lovely hand and the bomb under her arm.

Cornell pointed a shaking finger at it.

"B-b-b . . . " he stuttered.

"What, darling?" She handed him the packet. "Light us both a cigarette would you?"

"B-b-b . . . "

Cornell stopped trying to speak and fumbled the cellophane off the packet. He had a feeling, as he put two fags between his lips, that this was to be his last smoke.

He took a lighter from the table and lit the fags, his eyes popping as he watched Polly tear off the brown paper from the parcel.

Eventually he relaxed a little. The contents of the parcel was not a bomb. It was four big coloured sheets of card.

Cornell realised with a start what they were.

They were drawings.

Although twice the size of the comic, they were definitely pages from *Whoomf!*

He knew it because the sheets of card were actually four pages of the strip of The Devil Rider.

"Wh-what's that doing here?" he asked.

She looked surprised. "Why, it's just a comic strip delivered from one of my artists," she said. "For *Whoomf!* A good artist, isn't he? Almost as good as Laurence or Embleton, wouldn't you say?"

Cornell didn't know what she was talking about.

"The Devil Rider," he said thickly.

"That's right, darling. Do you read it?"

95

"No — I no . . . " He pointed at the big white spaces in the paintings. They were where the text would normally be. "Why isn't the writing there?"

"Because a letterer does that job. He fills in the words after the artist has drawn the pages."

"I see."

It was coincidence, of course. Polly couldn't possibly be mixed up in the affair, but it had succeeded in making Cornell extra jumpy.

"I must deliver these," she said thoughtfully. "They're two days late as it is."

"Wh-what about me?"

"Oh, Jerry, darling, I'm sorry — I've thought it all out. I know just where we can go where you'll be safe as houses. No one will find us. It'll be a lovely holiday for us, too ... "

Jerry Cornell felt a little more cheerful at this.

"Where is it?"

"I won't tell you. It'll be a surprise."

"Let's go, then."

"I'm sorry, darling — but I *must* make a call at Wayflete and another in Whitehall first."

"All right," he said passively. He was as good as dead anyway, he supposed.

Polly took her time getting dressed, but eventually she was ready. She wore a black corduroy blazer and a bright orange and blue mini-skirt, cream, patterned stockings and elegant strap-over shoes. She made Cornell feel like a bum.

It was fair enough, really. He *was* a bum.

They took her car — a 1958 Rolls Royce — into town. She drove while Cornell sat in the back, keeping his head down.

Polly eventually stopped the car outside the Wayflete Building.

"Don't worry, darling," she said, tucking the parcel under her arm. "Just a quick word with Barry Wharton and I'll be out again."

Cornell huddled on the floor and said nothing.

Polly was gone for an hour. In that hour Cornell sweated himself dry.

She hopped into the car and started it up.

"Sorry I was so long. I had to get something from the accountants and it took more time that I expected."

The car smoothed down Great Pie Street towards the embankment.

It turned off the embankment near Charing Cross and, from the floor of the Rolls, Cornell saw that they were going along Whitehall.

They stopped outside the Ministry of Defence.

Cornell guessed that Polly must be going to see John Brook-Hopkins about something. He saw her tuck a long flat envelope into her bag as she got out of the car.

"Keep cheerful, darling. We'll be out of London soon."

Cornell risked peering through the window. He saw her trip up the steps, her black Tom Jones bow bobbing, and enter into the dark confines of the ministry building.

Cornell waited even longer this time.

He began to feel that Polly had deserted him. Then he began to feel that she had come to harm. He started to worry.

He worried for quarter of an hour and then decided that he must look for her. She was all he had. She was his passport out of London, his chance of staying alive.

Then he could stand it no longer.

He wriggled out of the car and dashed across the pavement towards the Ministry of Defence. No harm could possibly come to him once inside the ministry, he was certain.

A doorman tried to stop him, but he pushed past and fled into the maze of corridors.

"Oi!" said the doorman. "Oi — sir!"

Cornell rushed blindly up a staircase and bumped into a girl bearing a tray of tea-cups. "Sorry," he said, "but can you tell me where I can find Mr. John Brook-Hopkins."

"He's just along the corridor," she said nastily, pointing with her tray. "Room 72."

Cornell made for Room 72.

Before he reached it someone came out of Room 61.

It was Fry with another man whose face Cornell vaguely remembered from newspaper pictures.

"Jerry!" Fry said in astonishment. "What are you doing here?"

"Cornell gasped and shook his head.

To Fry it looked as if Cornell was trying to tell him something secret. He murmured to his companion. The man nodded and moved away up the corridor.

"Now, Jerry," said Fry, taking his arm. "What are you on to?"

"I'm not sure, sir," Cornell said. "But I might have found out who your spy is."

"Good man! Who is it?"

Cornell saw Polly leave Room 72. She was walking down the corridor. She seemed abstracted and she plainly hadn't yet seen him with Fry.

"I can't talk now, sir. No time," Cornell said thankfully. "I'm on the job, sir. Don't worry."

"Good man!" Fry said again.

Cornell broke away from him and went towards Polly.

"Hello, Polly."

She looked up at him surprised.

"I thought you were going to wait in the car, darling," she whispered.

"I thought something had happened to you," he muttered. "Let's go, quick."

Fry rather ostentatiously pretended not to notice him as he led Polly to the staircase and descended.

Watching the two figures come down the outside steps of the Ministry of Defence from across the other side of Whitehall, Joseph K. gave a smirk of satisfaction.

"His offices must be in there," he said. "He has reported to his masters."

"What does that mean, comrade?"

"It means that he has said nothing or very little about us, comrade," Joseph K. said impatiently.

"How so, comrade?"

"Because we should have been arrested by now — he knows we are here, of course, but he has decided to play the game alone. What an opponent this Cornell makes! I have known nothing like it since the German, Herman Gorman, before the war. Gorman was like this Cornell — cool, ruthless, calculating — but a sportsman through and through. He would play his own game, in spite of what the authorities told him."

"What happened to Gorman, comrade?"

"Ha!" said Joseph K. He lept towards the waiting taxi. "Follow the Rolls," he told the driver.

"What happened to him, comrade?" Zhivako asked, needing reassurance. "To Gorman?"

"He runs a restaurant in Geneva, why?" Joseph K. asked.

Zhivako didn't quite know he felt the anticlimax to the anecdote so much. Perhaps he had wanted K. to recall how he had personally slit Gorman's throat, or something of the sort.

"You never caught him?"

"Oh, yes — I caught him and I let him go." Joseph K. said, peering ahead at the Rolls.

"Why?"

Joseph K. preserved his silence. He didn't want to tell Pyotr Zhivako that Gorman had offered him a half-share in the restaurant and that there was a very tidy sum from the profits deposited under a pseudonym in a Swiss Bank. Joseph K. had survived several changes of regime — but you never knew, did you?

The Rolls was heading North.

The taxi followed with some difficulty. Admittedly its bonnet hid a very powerful engine indeed, but it had been running for so long that it was beginning to tire a little.

Zhivako was also beginning to tire. He had had no proper sleep for nights. He sat back in the taxi and tried to catch up on his sleep.

CHAPTER EIGHTEEN

"IPSWICH," SAID CORNELL, noticing a sign as they drove through the town. "What are we doing in Ipswich?"

He was sitting beside Polly now. The sun was setting.

"It's on our way, darling. Don't worry. You'll be safe soon."

Cornell was beginning to worry. What if Polly were mixed up in this and she was taking him to his doom?

It was a silly thing to think, but then it was a wonder he could think at all in the state he was in.

The Rolls plunged on through the night, deep into the heart of East Anglia. The road was high, but below Jerry could see white mist hanging in the dales. He had never seen mist quite like it — so solid seeming and so white.

"Ipswich!" Zhivako said, waking from his fitful slumber. "Where is Ipswich, comrade?"

Joseph K. snorted. "It is immaterial. They are not stopping here. We will change drivers soon — you will drive. The man is getting tired."

Zhivako didn't really feel like being in the front seat. After all, if Cornell decided to turn like a wolverine he, Zhivako, would be the first to feel the bite of Cornell's fury!

Cornell the wolverine was trying to doze, but every time he did he had bad dreams. He dreamed that Shirley was pursuing him with a guitar from which bullets streamed. He dreamed that the Devil Rider (who was actually the corpse of Thorpe) was chasing him on a big black horse. He dreamed that Polly was strangling him with her long blonde hair.

All of the dreams were a little better than the reality he feared, but nonetheless he didn't think they were what you'd call light entertainment.

The Rolls turned into a side road after some time and the road got bumpy. Mist began to rise around them.

Eventually, at about three in the morning, the car stopped.

Polly turned towards him with a bright, sweet smile. "We're there, darling!" she chirped.

"Where?" said Cornell blearily.

"Our refuge — the place where no one will look for us, darling. A marvellous hide-out where we can be together."

Cornell tried to peer through the blanket of mist.

He shivered as she opened the door and the mist came in.

"We hide in the mist?" he said.

"No — the mist will go away. Come on."

Reluctantly he got out of the car and stepped into yielding mud. She took his hand and began to lead him across bumpy turf until they got to a plank.

Below the plank, Cornell heard the gurgle of water. The plank was slippery. He hesitated.

"Come on, darling."

She led him along the plank. He trod it gingerly.

They left the plank and stepped on to the deck of a boat.

It was a large cabin cruiser. Cornell realised suddenly that they must be on the Norfolk Broads. Maybe Polly's idea was a good one, after all. A boat — particularly a boat on the move — would be harder to get at than most things.

He began to cheer up as she led him into the big main cabin and lit the spirit lamps.

The cruiser was very plush. It had red plush, in fact, everywhere, and where it didn't have plush it had gilt and mirrors.

It was just like something luxurious out of Edwardian times, Cornell thought. It must have had a lot of money spent on it. But then Polly seemed to have a lot of money.

The commercial art agency business might be worth looking into, he thought, if there was ever a prospect of being able to get out of the spying racket.

"I'll make us some cocoa," Polly said deliciously.

"Lovely," said Jerry, leaning back on one of the plush bunks.

This was the life.

The cabin heaters that Polly had turned on began to warm the place up. If felt very secure. It was going to be idyllic, sailing along the Broads with Polly.

He hadn't had a proper holiday in years. He was going to enjoy this one, he knew.

CHAPTER NINETEEN

POLLY SEEMED TO change once she was on board the boat. Instead of being the sybaritic town girl, she had become the cheerful obliging country girl. She was up before Cornell and cooking him a huge breakfast almost before he was awake. He stretched in the wide, double bunk they had folded out the night before.

The sun was streaming through the cabin window. The smell of frying bacon and eggs was delicious. He yawned and smiled to himself slowly. All the cares of the previous few days were beginning to disappear.

"Ready, darling!" came Polly's rich, promising voice from the galley.

He rose and padded into the little dining cabin between the big cabin and the galley. The table was laid ready for them both. He sat down and tucked in.

After breakfast they went up on to the deck.

The sun was shining in a clear, pale blue sky. For miles around the flat, tawny countryside of Norfolk, with its winding, shining waterways stretched away. Here and there were the blackened outlines of old, abandoned farm houses and windmills. It looked like a part of England that had been untouched by time – as if it were still in the eighteenth century before the Industrial Revolution. Pieces of farm equipment had been forgotten and allowed to rust into the general background, rotting as an old tree might rot, returning to the dark earth.

Cornell and Polly lay together in a large, striped hammock swung over the deck.

It was a beautiful day.

There was no one in sight for miles. Not even a plane in the sky.

The boat rocked at anchor by the little pier and the occasional bird chirruped, but nothing disturbed their idyll.

Hidden in a thick clump of yellow rushes two men squatted uncomfortably. The ground was swampy and their shoes were full of water. They both looked very miserable. They were, of course, the dreaded Joseph K. and his unwilling assistant Pyotr Zhivako.

They watched jealously as the great Cornell disported himself not a hundred yards away.

He knew they were there, of course, but he didn't care. He was offering himself as a target. Coolly, he showed them how disdainful he was of their efforts to kill him.

No wonder Cornell had the reputation he had, Joseph K. reflected. There were few men who could lounge in a striped hammock, obviously absolutely relaxed, while leaden death threatened to scream from ambush at them at any moment.

Joseph K. drew his heavy Luger from his shoulder holster and thumbed the safety catch. His face hardened.

Pyotr Zhivako began to shiver, shifting his weight on his squelching feet and huddling down in the reeds as far as he could get.

Cornell had got out of the hammock now. He was ambling across the deck and then disappeared into the cabin. Joseph K. frowned, but kept his gun ready.

Polly had told Cornell that there was some fishing tackle below if he cared to try his hand at catching something for lunch.

He found the rod and came up on to deck with it, holding it awkwardly. He'd never fished before.

"I'll have a go, Polly," he said, "but I can't guarantee I'll catch anything."

"It's fun trying," she said.

He went to the rail and drew back the rod to cast the line over the side.

Joseph K. squinted down the barrel of his old-fashioned Luger, lining it up with Cornell's heart.

Cornell now drew back the fishing rod to cast the line.

Joseph K.'s finger whitened on the trigger.

Cornell cast the line, clumsily.

Joseph K. smiled. Cornell was as good as dead.

Then, quite suddenly, the gun was jerked from his grasp as if by some mystic agency.

It went flying through the air.

He heard it plop into the water some distance away.

K. goggled, even more amazed by Cornell's fantastic coolness. The man must have realised what was going on and deliberately hooked the gun out of his hand with the fishing line split-seconds before the Luger could fire!

His face a mixture of frustration and admiration, Joseph K. began to squelch back through the reeds on hands and knees.

Behind him Cornell whistled cheerfully.

"What happened, darling?" Polly asked. "Having trouble?"

"I think the hook caught on some reeds," he told her. "It's all right — it's free now."

He reached out and took the line. The hook looked a trifle bent.

"Hadn't you better put some bait on it?" Polly asked quietly'

"Bait? Oh, yes — of course. A worm or something." Cornell looked vaguely round for something to put on the end of the hook.

Peering at him from a safe distance through a pair of inferior binoculars, Joseph K. marvelled at how relaxed and unconcerned Cornell appeared.

The Russian investigator began to crawl through the mud, taking a wide detour around the boat, in the hope of finding his gun again.

It was a faint hope.

Polly was opening a tin of pilchards.

"Sorry, it's all there is for lunch, darling," she said. "But you weren't very lucky with the fishing, were you?"

Cornell shrugged.

"I wasn't really cut out for that sort of thing," he said, lounging back and watching her work on the pilchards in the galley.

"I'll go into the village later on and buy some provisions," she told him. "You'll be all right here until I come back, will you?"

"Right as rain," said Cornell comfortably. "This place is so peaceful."

They ate their pilchards.

Then Polly crossed the plank to the pier and got into the Rolls which was parked on the rutted, overgrown path that led to an almost equally rutted and overgrown road about half a mile back.

She waved cheerfully to him.

He waved back.

"I'll go for a walk, I think," he told her. "Along the bank. Is it safe?"

"Safe as houses — but mind the little plank bridge further up. If you cross it walk carefully — it tends to dislodge itself when it gets a bit slippery. You don't want to fall in."

"Okay."

He watched affectionately as she backed the car round and disappeared along the bumpy path.

CHAPTER TWENTY

CORNELL STROLLED ALONG the bank of the river whistling. He was clad only in a pair of brief bathing shorts. It was quite plain that he was unarmed.

Joseph K. lurking in the reeds not far behind decided that Cornell had become over-confident. He shifted the weight of the long marlin-spike into his right hand. The wicked barb of the thing was soon destined to plunge itself into Cornell's head.

As Cornell strolled, K. came sidling along the path of the river behind him, the marlin-spike poised. Behind K. came the reluctant figure of Pyotr Zhivako.

Zhivako was very nervous.

He was convinced that Cornell had something planned that would result in his (Zhivako's) and K.'s doom.

Cornell saw the little plank bridge that Polly had mentioned.

Whistling, he began to cross it, balancing himself by spreading his hands out on either side. The bridge was very unfirm and slippery, as Polly had warned him it would be.

Below was dank, weed-covered water.

It looked very deep.

Cornell went more carefully.

Polly had said something about steadying the bridge after he had crossed. Someone using it put it out of kilter every time.

But Cornell, never one to think of others very much, had forgotten her warning.

He stepped on to the opposite bank.

Joseph K., his face now flushed with rage and bloodlust, rushed across the plank, raising the marlin-spike to bring it crunching down on Cornell's skull.

The plank slipped.

It wobbled.

It slid slowly off the bank.

Joseph K. silently stood on it, his arms windmilling as he tried to keep his balance.

He dare not cry out in case Cornell heard him. He could only gasp and watch as the plank finally left the bank altogether.

With a huge splash, Joseph K. plunged into the stagnant water and disappeared beneath the weeds.

Zhivako, who had not started to cross the bridge, fled back into the weeds.

Jerry Cornell turned at the sound of the splash.

He saw nothing but the rippling water.

He decided that, against his experience of the morning, there must be some pretty big fish in the water after all.

He turned back and continued his leisurely stroll.

Seconds later, the purple face of Joseph K. appeared above the surface.

It was streaked with green weed. The hair was a mess of yellow scum.

But the expression on the face was one of even greater admiration for his opponent.

Cornell was playing with them. There was no question of it.

The man's legendary sixth sense had warned him on every occasion that Joseph K. had tried to kill him. He must be relying on that sixth sense.

Joseph K. began to lumber towards the bank, like a black hippopotamus that has failed to sink a canoe.

Zhivako helped him on to the bank.

"There must be some way," K. muttered. "There must be some way . . . "

Polly was gone longer than Cornell expected.

He didn't mind too much.

He had found some bottles of beer in the galley and was sinking these contentedly. He lay back in the hammock and looked at the lovely Norfolk sunset as it coloured the sky deep red and dark yellow.

He was all too unaware of the dark and dreadful doom that Joseph K. was planning for him.

The Russian investigator had decided that sudden assassination was impossible. Cornell's sixth sense warned him of the danger every time. The only thing to do was to construct a method of killing Cornell that would take some time.

That was why Joseph K. was stripped only to his black serge trousers, gripping a hand drill between his teeth and swimming strongly up river towards the boat.

His plan was simple.

He would begin drilling holes just below the waterline. Cornell and the girl would go to bed soon after dark. While they were asleep the boat would begin to sink. It would be down before they realised it — taking them with it.

If Joseph K. hadn't been gripping a hand drill between his teeth he would have smiled triumphantly.

The hull of the boat was quite close now. Soon he would begin work.

CHAPTER TWENTY-ONE

IT WAS GETTING quite dark, Cornell thought. He hoped nothing had happened to Polly.

She should have been back ages ago — unless something had cropped up, like the car getting a flat tyre.

There was no way of contacting her, of course, and she had no way of getting in touch with him. He would have to wait and drink beer and hope that she returned soon.

Joseph K., his head just above the water, prepared to sink the bit of the drill into the timber of the boat's hull.

He smiled coldly now that his mouth no longer was filled with drill.

He heard Cornell pacing around on the deck. When the woman returned the pair of them would go to bed. The boat would gradually fill with water and — that would be the end of the most feared agent in the western world.

Zhivako crouched in the reeds nearby, convinced that K.'s plan could not succeed. Eventually Cornell would stop playing with them — and pounce like a wolverine. It could be now.

Now would be a poetic time to know death, Zhivako decided. It was dusk. The mist was beginning to rise; the sky was deep purple, black and churned yellow as the sun set over the tawny waste of wild water and reeds.

Somewhere a fox barked. Elsewhere the voice of a petrel could be heard calling through the still air.

It was growing colder.

Zhivako watched his chief's head as it bobbed beside the boat. He saw Cornell begin to move across the deck, clutching a quart beer bottle in one hand.

Cornell paused by the rail, just above the spot where Joseph K. was madly drilling.

Cornell did not look down.

Cornell yawned and dangled the empty beer bottle out over the water. Another dead soldier. He thought he'd turn in for an hour or two to kill time while Polly was gone.

He let the beer bottle fall into the water.

At least — he thought he let it fall into the water.

Actually it fell on the large, round head of Joseph K. as he busily bored a hole in the boat.

Where there should have been a plopping sound as the bottle fell into the water, there was a sharp *thunk*!

"Ugh!" said Joseph K. letting go of the drill. "Uph!" He lay on his back and began to drift downstream.

The reason that he did this was quite a simple one.

He was quite unconscious.

Cornell, unaware of this, walked back towards the cabin, while Zhivako began to dog-trot along the bank, keeping pace with his floating master. Zhivako couldn't swim, otherwise he might have jumped in to the rescue.

As it was he paced the floating body in the hope that it would come to a bend in the river where it could be dragged ashore, or otherwise come to rest on a sandbank or something.

There was a bitter, bitter, bitter smile on Joseph K.'s features as if, even in this condition, he knew that the fiendish Cornell had defeated him once again.

Cornell was in the cabin. He didn't notice Zhivako or K. disappearing round the bend in the river.

But someone else did.

A woman dressed all in black from head to foot. She wore a black leather suit and a black leather helmet. Her eyes were masked by goggles and she wore black leather gloves and black leather boots.

114

In one gloved hand she held a black object with a luminous screen. A light winked at a point on the screen. It was an electronic tracking device of some kind. One of the latest gadgets that everybody had — except possibly the British Secret Service.

The woman consulted it and then returned her attention to the two men — the first in the river, the second beside it — peering at them closely while the light held.

She was very comfortable, lying on a black plastic inflatable mattress. At her hip was a 9 mm automatic in a belt holster. She had a broad belt around her waist which contained various compartments. Beside her lay a radio and various other pieces of equipment, including a heating unit which gave off no smoke or odour but which could cook far faster than any ordinary primus stove or wood fire.

Her field of vision did not take in Cornell. He was round the corner and the boat was hidden by tall reeds.

Had the woman arrived earlier and given herself time to look around, she would have found the boat easily enough but now it would not be until dawn that she would discover it.

She thought she recognised the young man running along the bank, but could not be sure. The old man who lay unconscious on his back drifting downstream, she had never seen before.

From one of the compartments at her belt she took a tiny but useful micro-camera and snapped several shots of the two men. Then she put the little camera away.

There was nothing more she could do tonight.

She stretched back on the mattress and went to sleep.

CHAPTER TWENTY-TWO

JERRY OPENED HIS eyes and blinked. He felt tired.

It was pitch black in the cabin. He wondered how long he had slept.

He got up and put on one of the little lamps. It burst into warm flame.

He glanced at his watch.

That was odd. It was two o'clock in the morning and Polly wasn't back. Something must have happened to the car. He began to worry.

He decided to go up on deck and see if he could make out any sign of her.

Clambering up the companionway he saw that it was actually very dark indeed. Only the white mist that hung over the Broads could be seen.

It was very cold.

Cornell shivered.

He wondered how Shirley was and what Fry was doing. He began to feel quite nostalgic for London. He was the sort of man who was only happy, when it came down to it, with fifteen miles of built up area in all directions.

With Polly to take his mind off it, he had enjoyed the sense of isolation in a way. But now — with no Polly — it began to bother him.

Suddenly the night was split by a chilling scream.

Cornell started and stared around, unable to see anything in the swirling white mist.

The scream came again. It was not a scream of pain. Rather it was a defiant scream. A maniac's scream.

The scream turned into a wild, cackling laugh.

Cornell heard the thump of hooves over the turf.

He shivered the more – this time not from cold.

He thought he made out a dim, grotesque silhouette of a rider on a huge stallion galloping away to his right.

Then there was silence.

Only the lapping of the cold water against the side of the cruiser could be heard.

Cornell wished that he had a weapon of some kind. He wished that he had brought his gun. He very rarely carried a gun on the old assumption that if he had one someone else might feel the need to use theirs.

In this case, however, someone was already using theirs.

He stood by the rail of the boat, frozen by fear.

He heard the distant sound of hooves again, galloping rapidly over the mushy ground.

Again the horrible, caterwauling laughter.

Then he saw him.

He could hardly believe his eyes as the horseman came plunging out of the swirling mist.

It was the character from the comic strip – from the Devil Rider strip in *Whoomf!*

It was the Devil Rider himself come to life. The face was covered by the bizarre mask, with its grinning head, its mad eyes and the horns curling upwards on both sides of the head. A heavy scarlet cloak spread out behind it and the black stallion's eyes seemed to gleam red and terrifying.

Cornell remembered suddenly that the Devil Rider in the strip was supposed to haunt the wilds of East Anglia.

He also remembered how Thorpe had died – the victim of a ritual killing. Thorpe had been murdered by devil worshippers.

It all fitted together neatly.

Cornell realised that he'd been suckered good.

Someone connected with *Whoomf!* was not only the spy who was passing secrets to the Russians. He was also connected with the devil cult and doubtless wrote the Devil Rider strip. He had been lured out here by a member of the cult — which was also a spy ring.

He realised who had lured him.

He realised why Polly Snapgirdle had been at the Secretary Bird club that night. It was to get him and somehow bring him out here where he could be murdered the way Thorpe had been murdered.

Cornell began to cry.

CHAPTER TWENTY-THREE

WHEN HE HAD finished crying, Cornell began to mewl in terror.

He scuttled down into the cabin and slammed the door shut, bolting it.

That was why Polly hadn't returned. She had done her job. Now it was up to the other members of the devil cult/spy ring to get him and kill him.

As he backed into the cabin another realisation struck him.

His feet were wet.

He looked down.

The floor of the cabin was awash with water.

The cruiser was sinking!

His enemies had done their work well. They had left him no avenue of escape.

Cornell didn't know that it was not the devil cult but the Russian investigator Joseph K. who had holed the boat.

He had only managed to drill two small holes and the cruiser might be water-logged by morning but it certainly would not sink.

Cornell, however, was unaware that it would not sink. Even now he saw himself drowning.

He opened the cabin door again and went out on to the deck.

There was no sign of the Devil Rider now.

Stuttering in terror, Cornell rushed across the gangplank and began to run up the rutted path towards the road.

His one hope was to reach the main road before they got him. But he didn't give himself much of a chance. He could hear the reeds rustling and it seemed to him that every clump held a grinning, wicked face full of insane bloodlust.

He heard the thump of hooves again. Heard the wild, crazy laughter of the masked horseman.

This was worse than nightmare.

Stumbling along the path, Cornell fell flat on his face. He got up and ran on, but fell again within a few minutes.

The path got bumpier and bumpier. At last he realised that he was no longer on it all all. He had lost it.

Everywhere was mist.

He had no idea in which direction he road lay, but his legs kept moving and he kept running like a headless chicken, his mind a quivering vortex of fear.

Now the sound of hooves was closer. The ground shook. He heard the snort of the horse, the giggling of the madman who drove him on.

He fell again and felt the air rush past him as the insane horseman leapt his stallion over his head and disappeared into the mist.

The Devil Rider was enjoying his hunt, thought Cornell dramatically.

He got up and began to run in the other direction, aware that the Devil Rider was playing with him as a cat played with a mouse.

Another figure loomed up in front of him. He bumped into it.

"Jerry, darling! What are you doing out here?" said the figure.

On his knees, Cornell stared up into the dimly seen face of Polly Snapgirdle.

She was mocking him, he felt sure. He *knew* she was one of them!

"L-let m-me g-go . . . " he begged. "I d-don't know

122

anything. I swear. Not a thing. If you let me go I won't be able to tell them anything . . ."

"Tell who?" She seemed genuinely puzzled. "I'm sorry I'm so late. The car got a puncture before I could reach the village. The nearest garage was twenty miles away. I had to get the bus there to bring them to the car — and they wouldn't come immediately. It's takes ages. As it was I had to leave the car at the garage!"

He looked at her hopefully, pathetically.

"Y-you're not lying to me, Polly?"

"Lying? Why should I?"

"I thought you'd lured me here so that the Devil Cult could get me."

"Devil cult, darling? What devil cult?"

"D-didn't you see him — the Devil Rider?"

"You must be in a bad way, sweet — that's the character in a comic strip. He doesn't really exist. You must have had a nightmare."

Cornell shook his head numbly.

"Come on," she said. "Let's go back to the boat. I've got lots of nice things to eat now . . . "

He remembered suddenly . . . . .

"The boat's sinking," he said. "They did it to get me off it."

She smiled sweetly and stroked his head. "Don't be silly, darling. Come on, I'll take you there."

She led him along the path back to the jetty.

It was only when she put her foot on the gangplank that she frowned.

"That's funny — there does seem to be something wrong with the boat."

She walked warily along the gangplank.

"D-don't l-leave me," Cornell begged.

"I'm just going to have a look below," she said.

She came back in a few moments.

"You're right," she told him. "The boat is sinking. Who

could have done it?"

"I t-told you — the d-d-devil cult . . . "

Cornell 's fear-sharpened ears picked up the sound again. The sound of hooves as the great, black stallion returned.

The ground shook. Polly gripped his arm.

They watched in horror as the Devil Rider, his laughter echoing through the mist, appeared some distance away and was gone again.

"Fantastic!" Polly said. "Absolutely fantastic! I say, darling, this is a thing, isn't it?"

Together, they began to run like mad.

CHAPTER TWENTY-FOUR

POLLY AND JERRY ran along the bank of the river, plunged across the plank bridge and began to push their way through the clumps of tall reeds that could be felt rather than seen in the clinging mist.

The air seemed filled with the sound of hooves and the Devil Rider's maniac laughter.

Polly and Jerry ran as fast as they could. Jerry was incapable of thought on his own. It was Polly who led the way.

Suddenly they stumbled into a little clearing and tripped over something.

The something grunted and began to stand up.

Cornell stood there looking wildly at the apparition. Dimly he made the shape. It was a big bulky man of foreign appearance, swathed in a huge, weed-covered black overcoat.

"Uh?" said the apparition.

"Uh?" said Cornell.

"Who on earth are you, darling?" Polly asked in surprise.

Another figure rose. Cornell, incapable of movement, simply stood his ground, convinced that these were more minions of the Devil Rider.

"So — Mr Cornell! We are face to face at last," wheezed the bulky figure of Joseph K. "May I compliment you. Presumably you have come to deliver the *coup de grâce*. Well — I am ready. So is my friend.

"I had nothing to do with it," said his friend.

Cornell recognised the friend as the private detective. He was astonished.

"I thought I told you to lay off," he told the private detective, forgetting his fear for a moment.

"I intended to . . . " said the other apologetically. "But my chief here — he insisted . . . "

"Coward!" Joseph K. hissed, turning to him. "Traitor. Revisionist!"

"We are all revisionists now, remember, comrade?" Zhivako reminded him gently.

"Stalinist, then!"

Zhivako looked hurt.

Joseph K. turned back to Cornell.

"You win, Mr Cornell. I am ready to meet my end. I am the loser. But remember that whatever you do to me, the cause continues. That has destiny on its side. Destiny you cannot destroy as you destroy one of its minions."

Cornell gaped at Joseph K., completely unable to understand what the man was talking about. He noticed that it had started to drizzle.

"Unless you would be interested in a quarter share in a very thriving restaurant in Geneva . . . " Joseph K. added "It's making a fortune — all Swiss francs, too."

Again the ground began to shake.

Again came the wild, maniac laughter of the Devil Rider.

Polly tugged at Cornell's hand. They ran on.

It seemed to Joseph K. and Pyotr Zhivako that Cornell and his companion had melted into the night. They only half-heard the sounds of the Devil Rider.

Joseph K. smiled to himself. It reminded him of the old days and the deal he had done with Gorman which was now so profitable to them both.

Cornell must have decided to accept the offer. There were now three partners in the restaurant in Geneva. Fate made strange bedfellows, he thought.

Polly and Cornell plunged on as they heard the sound of the Devil Rider coming closer and closer.

They were badly out of breath, but there was nothing for it but to keep running.

This time it was Polly who, with a little scream, slipped and fell.

"A log!" she said.

"What the ——?" said a new voice.

Out of the mist rose yet another figure. This one was all in shiny black.

Cornell gulped. The face was masked by a huge pair of goggles that had seemed at first to be the eyes of some monstrous insect.

It was the Woman in Black who stood before them.

CHAPTER TWENTY-FIVE

THE WOMAN IN Black said nothing. She stood looking at Jerry and Polly with one hand on her hip, just near the butt of her 9 mm automatic.

Jerry and Polly backed away, certain that she was connected with the Devil Rider.

The Woman in Black opened her mouth to speak.

With a shriek of terror, Jerry grabbed Polly and they began to run again.

Soon the Woman in Black was behind them. Cornell had never realised that the Broads could be so full of people.

Now the Devil Rider was approaching again. The horse snorted and whinnied. Its hooves thumped over the ground.

The Devil Rider's chilling laughter rang in their ears.

Nearer and nearer it came until——

——*It was on them!*

The huge stallion leapt over their heads. The horseman wheeled, blocking their path.

"Yaaa-haaa-haaaa!"

Panting, Polly and Jerry could run no further.

"So, you seek to flee the Devil Rider, little mortals!" said the Devil Rider in cold, mocking tones. "You will learn that he cannot be escaped."

"We haven't done anything," Cornell said weakly.

"Have you not?" The Devil Rider laughed again. "Have you not?" The horse snorted. "I say that you have and that you will suffer the Devil Rider's terrible justice!"

From all around them now came masked figures. All wore the half-masks of devils, just as the Devil Rider's helpers in the comic strip wore masks.

Cornell and Polly clung together.

"How horrible!" said Polly. "How perfectly nasty, darling,"

The clammy hands of the Devil Rider's minions fell upon them and they began to be bundled along towards the outline of what had appeared from the distance to be only one of the many ruined and deserted windmills that dotted the Broads.

Eventually they got to the windmill and were pushed through the creaking door.

Inside a torch guttered and they saw rats scuttle away.

"It's *exactly* like the strip!" Polly said in surprise. "How *camp*!"

"Silence!" said the Devil Rider as he led his horse into the mill. He reached out with a gloved hand and pulled a lever in the wall.

Part of the floor suddenly opened up and they saw a ramp leading down into a vast cellar below.

Cornell's legs gave out then and he fell forward in a faint.

CHAPTER TWENTY-SIX

WHEN CORNELL WOKE up it was to find himself spread-eagled in chains against a stone wall. Polly was beside him, also spreadeagled.

Standing before them, his hands on his hips, his grotesque masked faced looking up at them, was the Devil Rider.

"What's all this about?" Cornell said feebly.

"You know very well, you cowardly dolt!" the Devil Rider rumbled. "You are here to have justice meted to you."

"What have *I* done?" Cornell asked, his voice rising in justifiable outrage.

"Murder!" said the Devil Rider theatrically.

"Murder? But I've never killed anyone — well, hardly anyone. What's it got to do with you anyway?"

The Devil Rider's maniac laughter echoed through the dank dungeon.

"So! You deny that you killed Judy Judd and Henry Fairbright?"

"Who me? Killed them? Don't be soppy — you killed them!" Cornell said.

"Killed two of our own kind! Your lies are paltry!" The Devil Rider told him, striking a new attitude by folding his arms over his chest.

"This is ridiculous," Cornell muttered, wriggling in the chains. "Let us go." Then he added, with some curiousity, "What do you mean — 'two of your own kind'?"

"Two fighters for justice — two members of the Devil Rider's entourage. You know very well what I mean," the Devil Rider said.

"Oh," said Cornell. "They were in the cult, were they?" If he sounded inane it was because he was pretty inane. His fear had left him with an odd feeling of euphoria. He couldn't believe all this was happening. It was too crazy for something like this to be going on — straight out of the pages of a kid's comic.

Then he remembered Thorpe and shuddered.

"You'd better let me go!" he threatened.

"Why so? So that you might not get your just deserts?"

"You killed Thorpe, didn't you?" Cornell said. "Didn't you?"

"Thorpe? Who was Thorpe? We have killed no one — until now!"

Cornell glanced at Polly. Her face was very pale. She seemed to have changed. Her expression had become hard and desperate. She didn't seem to be the same woman.

"Then who did kill Thorpe?" Cornell demanded. "If you didn't?"

The Devil Rider turned away and began to stride about the cellar. He seemed somewhat overweight, underneath the fancy dress. He didn't look nearly so terrifying on foot as he did on horseback.

He wheeled suddenly and dramatically, pointing a finger at Polly.

"Possibly she killed this Thorpe, too," he snarled. "As she killed Judy Judd and Henry Fairbright."

"Who killed Judy Judd and Henry Fairbright?" Cornell asked in amazement.

"She killed Judy Judd and Henry Fairbright," said the Devil Rider.

"I killed Judy Judd, Henry Fairbright and Thorpe," Polly said, "darling I'm awfully sorry, but I simply had to. I wasn't going to kill you, Jerry. You were so sweet — and a perfect love. You're too *thick*!" She smiled at him affectionately. "I just wanted to find out how much you know — and how much you wanted to know . . . "

132

Cornell blushed. "I'm not thick," he said. "I'm just interested in self-survival. Why did you kill them?"

"Enough of this!" the Devil stormed.

"Don't pay any attention to him," Polly said. "He won't hurt us, Jerry. I suppose it wasn't fair of me to kill Thorpe so it looked like a devil-killing — but I had to throw everyone off the scent somehow. But you needn't worry about this lot — they're harmless."

"Silence!" said the Devil Rider raising a hand. "If you think we won't mete out our grim justice, you're jolly well wrong!"

"My god!" Cornell said. "It's . . . "

"That's right, darling," Polly told him. "It's Barry Wharton. He loves dressing up."

CHAPTER TWENTY-SEVEN

THE WOMAN IN Black had followed Cornell and Polly Snapgirdle after they had bumped into her. She had seen them captured by the Devil Rider and had trailed them to the old windmill.

Now she had opened the trap-door just a little and was peering through at the scene below.

When she saw Cornell and Polly spreadeagled in chains against the wall a thin smile crossed her lips.

She settled down to watch what happened.

The Devil Rider stamped his foot. "You're got to take this seriously. Miss Snapgirdle," he said. "We really do mean to kill you in some horrible way. Honestly. We've just got to think up a way, that's all. We'd have done it before if we could have worked it out."

The malevolent mask glared balefully up at them, but now that Cornell knew it was Barry Wharton behind it, he didn't feel quite so frightened.

"They come down here every weekend," Polly was explaining to Cornell. She shitted uncomfortably in her chains. "The whole staff of *Whoomf!* and some of the other people in Wharton's department. They play at Devil Rider all weekend and then go home again. It's a harmless enough fantasy."

135

"But why did you kill Judy Judd and Henry Fairbright?" Cornell asked with interest.

"For the same reason that I killed your friend Thorpe, darling." Polly told him with a sigh. "They'd all found out who the script-writer on the Devil Rider strip was – or rather Judy Judd and Thorpe did. Henry Fairbright saw me leaving Judy Judd's office after I'd fixed up her type-writer to go bang in her face." Polly laughed sweetly. "Oh, dear, what a job *that* was, darling."

"Who is the script-writer...?" Cornell began, but then blanched as a door at the far end of the cellar opened and two of the Devil Rider's minions came in wheeling a large brazier full of red-hot coals. "Oh, my god – did you say they were harmless, Polly?"

"They must be further round the bend than I guessed, darling," Polly said weakly. "You never can tell with these types, can you?"

Barry Wharton/the Devil Rider chuckled harshly.

"There, I told you you were jolly well wrong about us. We can do anything we like here and no one the wiser. Anyway it's only fair – it's our turn to murder you."

"I had nothing to do with it!" Cornell yelled. "Don't you realise that? It was all her – I was going to be a victim if she found I knew too much. Didn't you hear her?"

"A wizard wheeze, old boy," said the Devil Rider, taking an iron from the brazier, "putting on that act for our benefit – but we know you're as mixed up in this as she is. I say – doesn't it glow!"

"Let us go!" shrieked Cornell as the glowing iron came nearer and nearer.

He began to writhe in his chains. The rattle of metal against stone echoed through the cellar.

The Devil Rider paused and flung back his head. "Oho!" he said. "So you cannot take your punishment, eh? Ye're a cowardly rogue, too, to boot!"

"Stop this charade!" Cornell said. "You're like a lot of

kids!"

"There's nothing wrong with kids," the Devil Rider said seriously, pausing and lowering the iron. "You can learn a lot from kids. Kids are wiser than adults in many ways . . ."

"Then I suggest it would be wise to unlock these chains, darling," Polly suggested as Barry Wharton once again began to advance.

"You jolly well shut up, Miss Snapgirdle," Barry the Devil Rider said pettishly. "You've caused a lot of trouble just recently."

He looked down at the iron. During the conversation it had cooled.

He flung it down and stamped his foot again.

"Bother!"

Cornell cleared his throat and tried to speak, but it was difficult.

"Aren't you anything at all to do with the missing secrets from Whitehall?" he said, mainly to keep some sort of conversation going.

"Secrets? I don't know what you mean," Wharton said, stopping to pick up the iron and replace it in the brazier. "We're not spies here. This isn't a spy game."

"Mine is." Cornell said. "I'm a secret service agent. Honestly. It was my job to track down the people who were somehow managing to get secrets out of the country – we thought they were using your comic in some way."

The Devil Rider/Wharton chuckled icily. He certainly had the part off, thought Cornell.

"You can't fool us with a whopper like that," he said. "Though, come to think of if, why did you do what you did to Judy Judd and Henry Fairbright?"

"I didn't do anything to them," Cornell insisted.

The Devil Rider stirred the iron in the brazier. It had become hot again – white hot. He withdrew it and turned on Jerry.

"You don't half fib," said the Devil Rider. "I'm going to teach you a lesson for that. I'm going to *hurt* you!"

And with an absolutely paranoiac scream of laughter, the Devil Rider leapt towards Cornell.

Jerry fainted again.

CHAPTER TWENTY-EIGHT

IT WAS THE crash that woke Jerry up.

He blinked vaguely at the sight of the red-hot coals flying over the floor. He couldn't have been unconscious for long, because Barry Wharton still had the iron in his hand and was turning round to stare too.

It was the Woman in Black. She was flinging the two masked men into a corner while kicking the brazier with her foot.

Then she leapt at Wharton.

He yelped as she came at him. His bizarre mask fell backwards over his head and his eyes were terrified.

The Woman in Black seized him in a judo hold and flung him over her shoulder.

Two more of the Devil Rider's assistants came running at her. She banged their heads together and they fell down.

There didn't seem to be any more of them around.

The Woman in Black dusted her hands and drew her 9 mm automatic from its holster.

With some panache, she waved it at Barry Wharton and Co.

"The keys," came her clipped, decisive voice. It was faintly familiar to Cornell. "Come on, Wharton – the keys."

Reluctantly Barry Wharton felt among his robes and produced the keys to the manacles.

The Woman in Black strode over to him and flipped them from his shaking hand. Then she strode back to where Cornell was spreadeagled and undid him.

He fell forward on his face and groaned.

The Woman in Black helped him to his feet.

"Th-thanks," he said. "I think."

"What do you mean — you think?" said the clipped voice authoritatively.

"Well, I don't really know whose side you're on, do I?" said Cornell, pedantically in the circumstances.

"No, that's right," said the Woman in Black.

There was a rattling sound behind them.

They turned.

Polly Snapgirdle had somehow got hold of the keys from Cornell's chains and released herself.

She was haring up the ramp.

"Stop, or I shoot!" cried the Woman in Black, waving her gun.

She levelled the automatic as Polly reached the top of the ramp.

She squeezed the trigger.

Nothing happened.

"Damn!" muttered the Woman in Black. "Cheap caps!"

She re-holstered the gun and began to run after Polly.

Cornell followed. The Woman in Black made him feel safe. Besides, he had no wish to stay with the infuriated Barry Wharton and Co.

Polly was haring away from the mill. It was dawn. She must know the countryside of these parts very well, for she was zig-zagging expertly along.

Cornell and the Woman in Black found it hard to make her speed. They kept falling into pools of stagnant water or getting their feet stuck in mud.

The Woman in Black shouted: "She's making for that car!"

The car in question stood in a side-road about three hundred yards from the mill. It was a black Volkswagen.

It probably belonged to Barry Wharton. And he had

left the keys in the ignition. They saw Polly slam the door and start it up.

"Come on," said the Woman in Black. "There's a car just over there, on the other side of the hillock."

They ran up the hillock, topped it and looked down.

"Hey!" Jerry said in astonishment. "That's my car."

It was, indeed.

It was his Armstrong-Siddely. How had it got here of all places?

CHAPTER TWENTY-NINE

THE WOMAN IN Black got into the driving seat and expertly turned the car.

Soon they were bumping rapidly along the road that Polly had taken. They could still see her Volkswagan ahead of them.

Cornell was muttering to himself. He was thoroughly confused. There was no doubt about the interior of the car being the one he was most familiar with. How had the Woman in Black come to have it with her?

Within minutes they had turned off on to a larger road and, a quarter of an hour later, were on something that resembled a main road. At least it had a surface of sorts.

The Armstrong-Siddely picked up speed.

They zoomed through the twisting lanes in the early dawn light, but the Armstrong-Siddely, which needed servicing, was labouring a little.

They managed to keep the Volkswagen in sight, however. It probably had a special engine to go as fast as it did. Typical of Barry Wharton, thought Jerry.

They whizzed through Ipswich.

"She's heading for London, definitely," said the Woman in Black grimly.

Cornell turned and tried to make out what the Woman in Black looked like, but the goggles and the leather scarf across the lower part of her face made it impossible.

She drove very well, he noted. Better than him.

They went through Brentford at something of a lick. They were very close to London now and the Volkswagen was still in sight.

"Who are you?" asked Jerry at length.

"Can't you guess?" said the Woman in Black with a grim smile (it seemed to be a grim smile as far as Cornell could make out through the leather scarf).

"No," Cornell said. "You can't be Judy Judd — she's dead. You can't be Shirley. You can't be Polly Snapgirdle, because that's who we're chasing."

The Woman in Black said nothing.

They drove into London. Polly's Volkswagen was making for West London. Eventually she pulled up outside a familiar house in Ladbroke Road and jumped out.

"That's Dyescheoffsky's house!" Cornell said. "What does she want there?"

Polly was already walking through the front door as they piled out of the Armstrong-Siddely and ran up the path. Somehow the Woman in Black was supplying Jerry with the dynamic he normally lacked. He was so confused he wasn't even frightened any more.

The Woman in Black got her foot in the door just before it closed.

They tumbled into the house. A servant, looking bleary-eyed, mumbled something.

"Where did she go?" the Woman in Black harshed

The servant shook her head.

"Where did she go, man?"

"Uh!"

The Woman in Black drew her 9 mm automatic and waved it at the servant. He looked offended.

"It's only a cap gun," he said, pointing at it. The Woman in Black put it away.

"Where did she go?"

"Upstairs," said the servant sourly.

They rushed upstairs. They heard a muffled sound coming from one of the rooms.

The Woman in Black opened the door and they saw Polly Snapgirdle strangling Dyescheoffsky. He had hardly

144

woken up. He wore a silly smile on his face as he looked into Polly's lovely eyes.

The Woman in Black stepped forward and laid a hand on Polly Snapgirdle's shoulder.

"Unhand him at once," she crisped.

Polly Snapgirdle frowned. "I've got to kill him, darling. He knows too much," she said reasonably.

The Woman in Black put her arms round Polly's waist and began to heave.

Polly let go of Dyescheoffsky's throat and fell backwards. They began to roll around on the carpet, fighting.

Eventually Polly lay still.

The Woman in Black got up. "We'll deliver her to Det. Insp. Arthur Crapper, I think," she said.

Cornell sat down on the bed.

"Oof!" said Dyescheoffsky, moving his feet. "Is this anything to do with John Brook-Hopkins?"

"It might be," Cornell said systeriously.

"Ah!" said the Woman in Black. "So that's it!"

Cornell had really known it all along, but he had been suppressing it. He hadn't wanted to know. He really hadn't. John Brook-Hopkins was obviously the spy. There was no one else it could be. Jerry had tried not to think about it in case it got him into danger inadvertently.

"You could get his address at Polly's house I should think," he told the Woman in Black. There was no point in getting involved himself. She seemed to have the situation under control.

The Woman in Black picked Polly up and threw her over her shoulder. "Come on, then," she said.

"Um," said Jerry.

He turned to Dyescheoffsky.

"You were the one who was passing the stuff on to Moscow, I suppose," he said.

"Yes," said Dyescheoffsky. "Through the comic, I suppose all that's over now?"

"I suppose it is," said Jerry uncertainly. "Still, something else will turn up."

"It always does," said Dyescheoffsky.

Jerry followed the Woman in Black from the house. The Woman in Black bound and gagged Polly and popped her in the big boot of the Armstrong-Siddely.

They drove to Chelsea.

When they pulled up outside Polly's house, they saw the green Mini Cooper outside the door.

"He's here," Jerry said, pointing at the car. "The bloody poet — he's here!"

"Fine," she said.

"Supposing he's armed," Jerry said. "I mean — he'd try to kill us wouldn't he?"

"If you're worrying about me," said the Woman in Black, "don't."

Cornell was worrying about himself, of course, but he shrugged and followed the Woman in Black as she clambered over the low wall at the side of the house. They found themselves in the back garden.

Expertly, the Woman in Black forced open the french windows and they entered Polly's pretty house.

Cat-footed, they moved up the stairs to the main living room. The Woman in Black flung the door open and there was John Brook-Hopkins going through Polly's bureau.

"Good gracious!" he said.

He ran to the open window and went straight through. There was a balcony beyond it. As they chased after him, they saw him climbing down the drainpipe. He dropped the last few feet and began to sprint towards his car.

At that moment a taxi rounded the corner. In it sat two very tired Russians. The thickset one poked his head out of the windows.

"Ah! Mr Cornell — I've been looking for you."

"Stop him!" cried the Woman in Black. "Stop him!"

146

Joseph K. acted instantly. He sprang from the taxi with a skill born of long practice and threw his heavy hawthorn stick. It hit John Brook-Hopkins on the back of the head and laid him low.

Cornell and the Woman in Black went back into the street and stood over the prone John Brook-Hopkins.

The famous Poet of the Suburbs groaned and began to stir.

"I think that ties everything up," said Cornell grimly. "I'd better phone the chief."

He strode back into the house and picked up the phone.

Somehow it had all worked out very well. He congratulated himself that he would come out of this affair with some honour — and possibly even a rise.

CHAPTER THIRTY

JOSEPH K., PYOTR Zhivako, the Woman in Black and Jerry Cornell sat in Polly Snapgirdle's living room.

On the carpet in front of them lay Polly and John Brook-Hopkins, both bound and gagged.

"Well," said the Woman in Black. "I'm glad I was able to help a bit at the last minute. I expect you thought you'd had it that time, Jerry."

She tore off her leather scarf and goggles with a sigh of relief.

"Shirley!" said Cornell, "How . . . ?"

There were a lot of "Hows", and "Whys" and "Whos" as well.

"How did you know where I was?" he began.

"The usual way," she said mysteriously.

"What's that?"

"My secret," she told him. It was the way she always managed to trace him when he was off with his women. She had been convinced this time that he was off with one and she'd been right — only this time he had obviously been working on a case. There was a small tracer device which, some months ago, she had sewn into the shoulder-pad of his jacket. She wasn't going to tell him that though.

Cornell sighed and gave up.

Joseph K. rose from his chair. "Ah, Mr Cornell — about the business matter we discussed last night . . . "

Jerry didn't remember anything about a business matter.

Joseph K. took him to a corner of the room. "This is what I came to give you," he said. "That's why I was here in the first place. I thought you might have returned." He

149

handed Cornell a document. The document gave Cornell a quarter share in a thriving restaurant in Geneva. Jerry looked at it puzzled. Then he shrugged. He wasn't one to look a gift-horse in the mouth.

"I think we have an understanding from now on," said Joseph K. winking. "The other partner, as you no doubt know, is Gorman of course."

"Oho," said Jerry. "Gorman, is it?"

"The profits will be deposited in the Untermeyer Bank," K. whispered. "Under the name of Fox, if that is suitable."

"Fine," said Jerry. "Fine."

Joseph K. put one finger alongside his nose. "This is what we mean by international friendships, I think." He winked again and returned to his place.

Before Jerry could go and sit down, Pyotr Zhivako came up to him.

"Mr Cornell. I want to thank you," he whispered.

"Eh? What for?"

"For sparing my life . . . "

"That's all right," Cornell said grandly, wondering if the young man were insane. "I suppose you risk that sort of thing, being a private detective."

Zhivako smiled weakly. "Ha, ha!" he said. He was not sure what sort of subtle joke Cornell was making, but it seemed wise to laugh.

"I wondered," he began after a pause. He looked down at the floor, stirring the carpet a little with one foot. "You see – I thought you might be the person to help."

"What do you want?"

"I want to defect," Zhivako hissed suddenly. "I *need* to defect!"

Cornell looked at the wet lips, the shining eyes and knew he had a pervert on his hands.

"Okay," he said nervously. "All right – I'll help, don't worry."

"Thank you. Oh, thank you," Zhivako mumbled. He

turned to face Joseph K.

"Comrade," he announced, "I have defected. I have a full suit of fab gear in a left luggage locker in Leicester Square Tube Station — *and I don't care!"*

Joseph K. shrugged. He didn't know how Cornell had managed to blackmail Zhivako, but one defection more or less wasn't bothering him at the moment.

Joseph K. got up, bowed, shook Zhivako's hand, patted his shoulder and said: "There's really no need for these gestures, young man. You could have learned, but still . . . "

He nodded to his partner, Cornell, and left the room just as Fry came in. Fry glanced in astonishment at the retreating back of Joseph K.

"Wasn't that Joseph K., the Fox of Bucharest?" he asked Cornell as he joined them in the room.

"I believe so,' Jerry said. "We have an understanding."

"Good man," said Fry. "Good man."

He looked down at the carpet at John Brook-Hopkins and Polly Snapgirdle.

"What's all this?" he asked.

Cornell smiled a grim little smile. "They're the people you want, chief," he said. "Your spies."

Fry came over and pumped Cornell's hand. "Oh, good man! How did you get on to them?"

"It's a long story, chief," Cornell told him, "but briefly it goes like this. The words we wondered about — the words Thorpe spoke before he died that sounded like 'its innards drip' — remember?"

"Yes," said Fry with bated breath.

"He was really saying 'It's in the strip.' The information was coded and in the dialogue balloons of the comic strip. John Brook-Hopkins was the script-writer. He had started off doing it just to make a living, but Polly Snapgridle, his agent, realised the possibilities. She got him to get top-secret information and write it into the comic strip he did every week . . . "

"But how did she make him do it?" Fry asked in wonder.

"Simple blackmail," Cornell said. "Brook-Hopkins was broke — that's why he started doing comic-strip work to begin with — and he needed to keep earning the money. But he also wanted to keep his fading reputation. Polly threatened to reveal to the world who the writer of the comic strip was unless he did what she told him."

"Devilishly clever," said Fry.

"Devilish," said Cornell with simple wit, "is the word. Somehow the information got out anyway. One or two people at Wayflete knew who the writer was. Polly decided, after she'd seen me going to Wayflete, that things were getting too hot. She bumped off Judy Judd as she had earlier killed Thorpe when he had got on to her. Henry Fairbright saw her on the scene of the crime and she had to do him in too. That's about the size of it."

"Incredible!" said Fry, shaking Cornell's hand again.

"I suppose it is," said Cornell thoughtfully.

Pyotr Zhivako presented himself to Fry. "Mr Cornell has said that he will help me defect," he said thickly.

"You're young Zhivako from the embassy aren't you?" Fry said in surprise. "Jerry's convinced you to come over to us, has he? I say, Jerry — damned good work!"

Cornell smiled and shrugged. "Think nothing of it, sir."

Shirley took his hand.

"Come on, Jerry," she said. "You must be tired after all that work."

"I am a bit," he admitted.

As they climbed into the Armstrong-Siddely, he said: "One thing that's bothering me, Shirley. How come you know all about judo and that?"

"I had to do something while you were away," she said.

"I see."

She drove the car towards Notting Hill.

"By the way," he said casually, as they pulled up outside the flat. "What do you tell all those women. What makes them so frightened?"

"Ah . . . " said Shirley, and guided him up the steps to the front door.

THE END